How This Book Came To Be

In the summer of 1993, a novel called *Reckless Angel* jumped off the bookstore shelves at me. I bought it, took it home, and fell in love with the writing of Maggie Shayne. As fate would have it, Maggie showed up on the GEnie RomEx online bulletin board almost immediately. Within a month, Maggie's second book hit the shelves, and I sold my first novel—ironically to Maggie's editor, who had had my manuscript long before I met Maggie.

In the summer of 1994, I met Maggie in person for the first time at a national writers' conference in New York City. I felt her presence when she walked into the lobby, something I hadn't been able to feel through my computer screen. Though nearly 2000 people attended that conference, Maggie and I ended up sitting together at lunches, standing together in line, and bumping into each other in the halls. I'm not an easy person to get to know, but Maggie and I hit it off like long-lost sisters.

After that, I would run into Maggie once every year or two at a writers' conference. Each time, it was as if no time had passed between us. We shared similar dreams of a time long ago when we wore loose robes in an ancient temple, our bare feet on cool stone floors. We had been sisters together—priestesses—on more than one occasion.

In the summer of 2000 at yet another writers' conference, Maggie and I sat on a balcony overlooking Washington, D.C. and talking of all the things we hadn't been able to discuss in email. I had started my own small press to publish my between-the-cracks novels. The first book had come out, and I had a shorter prequel planned. Meanwhile, Maggie had written an incredible novella, but in spite of her skyrocketing career and her history of writing cutting edge stories, this novella was too different for all the major publishers. Our stories shared many traits: Wiccan heroines, ethical dilemmas, personal sacrifice, and love. Even her hero and my hero's son had the same name.

And so was born *Witch Moon Rising, Witch Moon Waning*, two short novels in one book. This book is a labor of love and a written testament of our faith, our belief in each other, and our destiny to have found each other in this life. I am truly blessed to have Maggie as my friend and soul-sister.

Lorna Tedder
Beltane, 2001

D1384432

Witch Moon Rising, Witch Moon Waning

Two Novels

by
Maggie Shayne
and by
Lorna Tedder

Spilled Candy Books
Niceville, Florida USA

Witch Moon Rising by Maggie Shayne and
Witch Moon Waning by Lorna Tedder
Copyright 2001 by Margaret Benson and Lorna Tedder, respectively

Published by: Spilled Candy's Novel Teaching Tools for Wiccans
               Spilled Candy Publications
               Post Office Box 5202
               Niceville, FL 32578-5202
               Staff@spilledcandy.com
               http://www.spilledcandy.com

ISBN:1-892718-35-9 (disk and download version)
ISBN: 1-892718-33-2 (trade paperback)

Library of Congress Card Number: 2001087323
First edition

Cover Art copyright 2000 by Ravon of WitchWay

Spilled Candy Books is grateful to Ravon of WitchWay for the cover art and continuing support of Spilled Candy Books. We encourage you to visit Ravon's web site at http://www.users.drak.net/ravon/. Ravon's art truly is a form a worship.

Witch Moon Rising
by Maggie Shayne

Chapter One

Mirabella lifted her head, blinked her sleepy eyes, and found herself standing upright, bound to the pole at her back. She couldn't move. It was only as she tried that she realized her body was entwined by rough, fraying rope that twisted around and around her from her ankles to her shoulders. When she pulled against it, it seemed to grow even tighter, cutting more deeply into her flesh, until her legs and arms tingled. She went still and waited for the pain to subside, the blood to flow into her limbs once more. A chill wind whipped her hair and drew goosebumps in her flesh.

The sky was a series of brushstrokes in varying shades of grim. Black as coal up high, then a stripe of wet slate, and a slash of bruise purple. Lower still, the horizon lightened to a pearly gray haze. No stars. No moon. Somewhere beyond the horizon the sun struggled to rise, while the darkness conspired to keep it down. But the light won out, as it always does.

Bit by bit, the area around her became visible. Though the entire place was shrouded in creeping, silvery mists, she managed to strain enough to see. Herself first. Her body. With her head cocked downward at a sharp angle she saw that the garment she wore beneath the serpentine rope, was ragged. Barely more than a burlap sack with holes torn for her head and arms to poke through.

Sackcloth . . . ?

Her legs and feet were bare. She stood on an upturned wooden crate, and below it, around it, were mounds of brush, limbs, twigs, branches. Something was smudged over the skin of her legs and arms. Soot or ashes or . . .

Sacklcloth and ashes....

Something acrid hung in the air. A familiar scent she ought to know.

Gasoline?

She sucked in a breath, and it seemed the wind died all at once. Her hair fell down to shield her eyes, raven strands, uncombed and wild. Then slowly, she lifted her head upright again, squinting to see what was going on around her.

People. A crowd of them stood elbow to elbow, staring at her. Somber, oddly quiet, their faces grim. She blinked and realized she was in the park in the center of town. She made out familiar landmarks. The Ezra Town Hall was just beyond the crowd to her right, its white paint chipping, hand tooled sign swinging when the breeze picked up again. The road lay behind her. She heard a car going past but couldn't see it. To her left, the river tumbled by, oblivious to her plight. She could hear it tripping over stones and laughing at its own clumsiness. And in between, people. So many people.

Their stares were cold, she thought as her gaze skimmed them all. Then all at once, her attention was caught, riveted like a fly on flypaper, to one man. He looked more hostile than any of the others. His dark eyes stared right back at her, piercing her soul with their anger and condemnation. He stood directly in front of her, and he held her eyes with his. His jaw was clenched and hard. His hostility reached her in waves so potent she felt them like physical blows.

I'd kill you myself if I could!

She felt the words in her mind, very clearly, though he hadn't opened his mouth to speak them. God, what had she done to so infuriate that man?

She wanted to cry out but couldn't. She tried, but no sound emerged. As if fear had frozen her very breath, robbed her of her voice. She wanted to move, but the ropes held on too tightly for that. She could only move her head, and she did, swinging it from side to side, seeking help in that crowd of onlookers. But no one there would help her. And her desperate gaze returned again and again to that angry man in the front. Everyone else faded to background colors. He alone remained clear, vivid. His emotions. His hatred. As clear to her as her own name.

"Mirabella St. Angeline," came a disembodied voice. "You have been found guilty by a duly appointed court of the crime of teaching Witchcraft to a minor and contributing to her mental illness and subsequent suicide. For these crimes you have been sentenced to death by fire to be carried out this day at dawn. Do you have any last words?"

She searched the air for the source of that voice, but found no speaker. She tried to say something in her own defense, tried to shout her denial, tried to plead, to beg for her life. Her mouth moved, but no sound emerged. And the man in the front took a step closer, his fists clenched, tears standing unshed in his eyes, and he said, "Burn in hell, Witch. Burn in hell for what you did to my daughter!"

"May God have mercy on your soul," the other voice intoned.

She heard the flames even before she saw them. The snapping jaws and smacking lips of hungry fire catching sight of its next meal. Panic gripped her in hands of ice when she saw the people in the crowd, bearing torches now. Where they got them, she didn't know. They'd had none a moment ago. But now they had come to life, those somber, silent onlookers. Shouting, swearing, cursing her, they surged forward, hurling their torches and their hatred at her.

The flames spread, licking up the gasoline and following it around her in a perfect circle. And then they leapt higher, so high they blotted out everything else, a towering monster that gobbled its way closer. Merciless heat seared her face. And yet, cruelly, almost teasingly, the curtain of fire parted and closed again and again, giving her glimpses of the man. His eyes were still affixed to hers. She felt her skin roasting, blistering and peeling. Her blood boiled and hissed as it bubbled from her pores. Her flesh melted and fell away from her bones. Pain: she didn't feel it, she became it. The embodiment of burning, screaming torment. She wished for death. But death did not come.

The ropes that held her burned through, and she stumbled from the crate, a human torch, twisting and writhing through the pyre, kicking aside piles of burning brush, until she came to the area beyond it. And still she staggered forward, until she slammed bodily into the solid chest of the hateful man. Her hands twisted into the fabric of his shirt as she pled in silence for his help. For his mercy. And then his shirt caught fire as well. She could still see his face, his hard, cold eyes staring into hers through a fiery veil. Then the fabric tore, and she fell to the ground, and he fell with her. She was tangled in him, in his burning arms and legs, and the dancing flames. His mouth found hers, and he kissed her as they burned.

Gasping, her mouth wide with anguish and silent screams, Mirabella opened her eyes. She was not on fire. She was on her bedroom floor, the curtains from her window twisted around her body, the rod bent almost in half and lying across her legs. She closed one hand in her own hair, as she panted for breath, whispering "Oh, God, oh, God," over and over again. Her heart was pounding so hard it thrummed in her ears. She was burning up with an inexplicable fever and damp with sweat.

She tried to stand, shaking so hard she fell to her knees again, then managed to get up and stay there on the second try. She got untangled from the curtains, dropping the rod, dragging herself to her bathroom, and stepping into the shower even as she cranked on the knobs. She didn't even undress first. Just stepped into the too cold water and let it sooth the imaginary burns she could still feel. Cool the fever that had no physical cause.

The water soaked her, soaked her nightgown, chilled her skin. She braced her arms against the wall to hold herself up, and turned her face into the flow. And finally, when she felt as if she were breathing again and those phantom flames had been extinguished, she turned the water off.

She had never even tugged the shower curtain closed, she thought vaguely, lifting her head. From the corner of her eye, she caught a glimpse of her own reflection in the mirror on the other side of the small bathroom. Hair tangled and dripping, face flushed and wet. She turned to face the mirror fully . . .

. . . and went utterly still. A woman stood behind her in the mirror. A woman with auburn hair and deep blue eyes.

Mirabella spun around, her heart in her throat. But no one was there.

Heart racing, she kept looking from the mirror, to the

shower stall again and again, as she clambered out, grappled for a towel. She was shaking all over. "What that hell was that? What the hell . . . ?"

Fighting to catch her breath, calm her heart, she knew only two things, and she knew them with vivid clarity.

Whatever had just happened to her had not been a mere dream.

And she was fully awake now.

# # #

"Just what do you think you're doing, Rowan?"

Jonathon Hawthorne stood in the open doorway of his daughter's bedroom, his breath knocked out of him by what he saw. She sat in the middle of her floor, surrounded by a ring of candles, which were the only light in the room. Her legs were crossed, eyes closed. Some tribal drum beat pattered from her stereo system. She didn't open her eyes or react to his presence in any way, beyond the slight stiffening of her limbs.

"Dammit, Rowan, what have I told you about this garbage?" He strode into the room, hit the light switch first, the power button on the stereo second.

When he looked at her again, her eyes were open and furious.

For just a second he could have sworn he was looking at her mother. She used to get that same infuriated, offended, and slightly arrogant expression when he dismissed her farfetched beliefs as nonsense.

Unfortunately, he'd been right. Otherwise, Ashley would still be alive. And he was damned if he would stand by and watch Rowan start down the same delusional path her mother had traveled.

"Since when do you just walk into my room?" Rowan asked without getting up.

"Since I don't want my house to go up in flames. Put the damn candles out, Rowan."

"You're supposed to knock!"

"I *did* knock. You apparently thought it was part of the infernal pounding on that CD you had playing."

"That was ritual drumming by a group of Native Holy

Men. *Not* infernal pounding."

He pushed a hand through his hair. Rowan was every-thing to him. A mirror image of her mother, who had been every-thing to him, too. He just looked at her for a moment. At her deep burnished hair, endlessly long and perfectly straight; at her smooth, ivory skin; at her thick dark lashes that didn't need the enhancement of mascara in the least. Fourteen. Five-three. A perfect size two with a burgeoning figure he pretended not to notice. Not a little girl any more. A young woman. And he felt sorry for the men she would encounter in a few more years. She'd put them all on their knees without even trying.

Lately, Rowan had been pulling away from him. And he hated it, but didn't have a clue how to fix things. Damn Ashley for leaving him to raise their daughter alone. *She* would know what to do with a daughter who suddenly changed from a smil-ing dimpled little girl into a brooding, incommunicative young woman who dressed mostly in black and rarely spoke more than a sentence at a time to her parent.

She sat now, glowering as she used a gold plated snuffer to extinguish her candles one by one, not even looking at him. "So what's the big emergency, Dad?" she asked when she'd snuffed the last one.

"I . . . nothing. I just wondered if you wanted a ride to school."

She stared at him, lips thinning.

"Do you?"

"No. Anything else?"

He sighed. "Rowan, what were you doing in here, just now? With the candles and the drumming and–"

For the first time, a hint of a smile tugged at her lips. "I was talking to Mom. Or trying to, at least."

It brought him up short. Like a punch in the gut, it drove the breath out of him, and it took him a minute to get it back. He closed his eyes, shook his head slowly, and when he could get words out again, he said, "Honey, your mother is dead. You can't talk to her, and anyone who tells you otherwise is a con-artist and a liar."

Her huge, expressive eyes grew angry again. "Just because you don't believe in something doesn't mean it doesn't exist!"

He opened his mouth to shout back at her but closed it again. "Okay. I don't want to fight with you about this. Breakfast is on the table. Come downstairs and eat before you leave for school. All right?"

She pursed her lips. "Yeah. Whatever."

"Ten minutes."

He left her, closing the door behind him, then pausing in the hall to ask himself if he was doing anything right in any way, shape or form, where she was concerned. He'd read all the books out there for single dads raising daughters on their own. God knew there were enough of them. He'd listened to all experts, and he was still lost as to how to deal with the sudden, drastic changes in his daughter.

Downstairs in the sunny, mostly glass breakfast nook, he picked up the newspaper, sampled his oatmeal and waited for Rowan to show up, determined to have a non-confrontational conversation with her for once.

But the story that caught his attention did nothing to help along those lines. Another crime with "occult" stamped all over it had taken place overnight. Someone had butchered a house cat in the local cemetery and painted odd symbols on a headstone in its blood. It was the fifth pet to have been killed in an apparent ritual sacrifice this month. One of the kids being questioned, the story said, had been seen running from the cemetery when police arrived. No doubt the full details would be waiting on his desk when he arrived at work. Poor goddamned cat, he thought.

And he was supposed to allow his daughter to start poking around in this kind of bullshit? Incense and candles and spells and charms? No way. Not in this lifetime.

Rowan came into the breakfast nook. She wore a heavy chain around her neck and a choker made of leather. Burgundy lipstick, purple eye liner, black tank top and jeans.

Sighing, he laid the paper down. "Honey, what's wrong?"

She looked at him as if startled, her eyes the biggest, bluest eyes in the universe. She had unusually large pupils. It was common, he'd heard, in fair skinned, blue eyed girls. But he didn't think anything about her was common.

"What makes you think anything's wrong?" she asked.

"I don't know. You just seem to be going through some changes lately, and . . . well, it concerns me."

"It's called growing up, Dad." She put her attention back on her oatmeal.

"Is there anything you want to talk to me about? Anything going on at school or–?"

She met his eyes, her own looking impatient now. "I'm not taking drugs or having sex if that's what you're asking."

He felt his jaw drop. "No. That's not what I was asking," he stammered. "You're way too young for me to be worrying about those kinds of things."

She rolled her eyes. "Right."

"What's that supposed to mean?"

"Nothing, Dad. I gotta go. Tell the people on your happy little planet I said bye, will you?" She softened the words with a teasing wink.

"Very funny."

Rowan got to her feet and slung her backpack over her shoulder. She started to go, then sighed and turned back. "Actually, there is something I want to talk about," she said.

He almost grinned. She wanted to talk to him! Finally! He smothered the urge to smile ear to ear, put on a serious face, and said, "What is it?"

She drew a deep breath, as if for courage.. "Mom. I want to know everything about her."

"But honey, I've always talked to you about your mom. I think I've probably told you just about everything I know about her."

"No, you haven't," she said.

He held her gaze for only a moment. And then he had to look away. Shit. How much did she know?

When he looked at her again, her eyes were closed. "I see her in my dreams, you know. Especially lately. She was so beautiful . . . way more than she is in any of her pictures. I don't remember her being that beautiful."

"You were only four, honey. Don't feel bad for not remembering. And if you wonder how beautiful your mom was, all you have to is look in a mirror."

She opened her eyes. They were damp. "Really? You think I look like her?"

"More every day." He was getting a little tight in the throat himself.

Rowan licked her lips. "Dad, it's like she's trying to tell me something, but I just can't get what. That's why I've been trying to talk to her, when I'm awake, you know, but . . . well, so far, I don't think it's working."

He swallowed the dryness in his throat. "That's because it's not possible. I'm sorry, hon, but it's just not."

"I don't believe that. And I don't think Mom did, either."

She leaned down, and kissed his cheek. "But I'm going to be late if I don't get going. Sometime, though, Dad, you have to tell me about Mom. The stuff you haven't told me before. Okay?"

"Yeah. Sure." He said it softly, distracted, shaken. His daughter managed a smile, but he thought he saw doubt in her eyes. "I promise," he added.

"Okay," she said. She reached behind her to pull a set of headphones out of her backpack and snapped them over her ears.

He watched her go and made a mental note to call the school, set up conferences with some of Rowan's teachers. Maybe that would give him some insight into what was going on with her. There was that one teacher she was always talking about . . . Miss Saint A., Rowan called her. She was one of the only teachers his daughter ever mentioned in any positive sort of way.

Yes. Miss Saint A. He'd start with her. She might be just the person to help him wipe all this hocus-pocus nonsense out of Rowan's head once and for all.

Chapter Two

"I have to say, I agree with you, Mirabella. I don't think it was a dream either."

"What then?"

Mirabella sat across from her dearest friend, Gwenyth, at a round table in the back Gwen's shop. Between them, Tarot cards lay face up, spread out in familiar patterns. The shop was housed in the lower front portion of the oversized Victorian house Gwen had inherited from her great-grandmother. She lived in the rest of it. Along with whatever stray creatures wandered in looking for a place to rest or a solid meal. Gwen could never turn away an animal in need.

The front of the shop had a large bay window that housed hunks of uncut quartz and amethyst, an assortment of candle holders and incense burners, several pieces of pyrite from the stream out back, a stack of obscure looking books, and a black cat called Circe who was usually curled up, sound asleep. Circe was the first and the favorite of all Gwen's pets. The gold, gothic lettering on the door spelled "Gwenyth's Chamber" in a curving arch. Beneath it, in smaller block letters, was a list:

Occult Supplies
Tools of Divination
Herbs
Oils
Brews
Candles
Psychic Readings
by appointment only

The shop—and Gwenyth—fit into this small town about as well as a square peg in a round hole. Mirabella had always been much more discreet about her beliefs. She had to be. She was a teacher at the high school, for goodness sake!

"If it wasn't a dream, Gwen, then what was it?" she asked.

Gwenyth drew a deep breath and flipped over another Tarot card. She was a petite woman, with honey gold hair that curled untamed to her shoulders. She wore jeans and a black sweatshirt that said "Witch and famous" on the front in orange letters. And of course, there was the ever present pentacle on a chain around her neck.

"A warning," she said at last. "I think it was a warning. It's definitely not past life, though there are connections to one. It looks like . . . something in the future." She looked up from the cards, meeting Mirabella's eyes, and hers seemed worried. "Honey, have you been talking to any of your students about the Craft?"

"You think I'm insane? Of course not."

Gwenyth shrugged. "Well, I don't know then. You know, up until recently, Wiccans in Ezra Township have been left pretty much alone. The locals grate their teeth and roll their eyes and tolerate us. Barely. But the tide's shifting, Mirabella. It's getting dangerous out there."

Bella nodded. "I know."

"Maybe you don't."

Frowning, Mirabella said, "What do you mean?"

Gwenyth licked her lips nervously, and Bella could see she was debating whether to say anything more. Then she seemed to decide all at once. "I've been getting threats."

Mirabella sucked in a breath and widened her eyes. "What kinds of threats?"

Gwenyth got up from her seat at the table and walked past the row of pewter figurines to step behind the counter with the antique register on it. She drew a manila envelope from beneath the counter and slid it across to Mirabella. Bella opened it and took out the contents. Scraps of paper, entire sheets, some folded, some not. All basically bearing the same message. "We don't want Witches in Ezra Township. Get out while you still can." Some were more colorfully worded than others, but the gist was the same.

"How long has this been going on?" Mirabella asked.

"A couple of weeks. About as long as the spree of animal murders they've been attributing to this so-called occult group that's cropped up. The problem is, there is no occult group. I'm pretty well networked, and I'd know if there was. I haven't heard a thing. Either these nuts are from out of town or . . . or I don't know what to think."

"Why didn't you say something about these threats before, Gwen?"

She shrugged. "Didn't see what good it would have done." She licked her lips. "I've had an offer on the house, Bella. Mark Hayes from the real estate office is willing to give me a very good price for it."

"When did you go see him?" Bella asked, frowning.

"I didn't. He came to see me. Actually, it had nothing to do with business. He asked permission to do some fishing in the stream out back–way back in the April, and he's been popping in ever since. Says he's fallen in love with the place."

"But . . . you're not considering selling?"

Gwen shrugged. "I wasn't. But since all of this—yeah, I'm thinking about taking it."

"That's totally unlike you, Gwen. To give up and run away."

Gwen licked her lips. "I don't like the whole town thinking I'm into butchering innocent house pets and defacing hallowed ground in the cemetery."

"Nobody thinks that!" Mirabella shouted.

Gwenyth tilted her head to one side, frowning at Bella as if she were sprouting horns. "Honey, of course they think that! Who else are they gonna suspect? I'm the only Witch in town, so far as most people know. Everyone else is pretty much in the broom closet. To the locals, it's the natural conclusion."

The chimes over the door jangled, and both women turned around to see Billy Cantone, a man they'd both gone to high school with, coming toward them. He was wearing his uniform, star pinned to his chest, right over his heart. And he wasn't smiling.

"Well, hello Billy," Gwenyth said. "Dare I hope you're looking for a love potion or a good luck charm?"

He pursed his lips. "'Fraid not, Gwen. This is official business." He nodded at Mirabella. "Surprised to see you here, Bella."

"Shoot, Bella and I are old friends, Billy. We see each other quite often," Gwen said before Bella could say a word. Then she turned to Bella again. "I'm sorry I couldn't be of help to you. I know as a teacher you're as concerned as I am about this rash of nastiness hitting our town, but I really don't have a clue who's behind it."

She was giving her an out. Letting her keep her "cover" intact. Mirabella lowered her head and muttered her good-byes.

When what she wanted to do was look Billy in the eye and tell him the truth.

"You'd better go, Bella," Gwenyth said, glancing at her watch. "You hang around here any longer you may just lose your job." Then she tapped the watch. "You know how Sally Hayes hates her teachers showing up late.

"Yeah, well, she might forgive me if I tell her I was at her husband's favorite fishing hole. But you're right." She got the message loud and clear. She risked her job every time she came into this shop and would lose it for sure if she spoke her mind to Billy. Still, she was ashamed of herself as she turned and walked away.

But as it turned out, she didn't get all that far.

Rowan was deep in thought as she walked to school, and she shut the world out in her usual way–with her portable CD player blasting and her headphones firmly in place. Her body was changing. Her mind was changing. And things were . . . happening to her that she didn't understand. Her father didn't want to talk about it. Seemed almost afraid of it. But Rowan knew somehow, way down deep, that her mother would have understood. That she had gone through these very same things. That she'd had . . . something extra.

Just like Rowan had.

Reaching into her jacket pocket, Rowan fingered the small woven pouch she'd found tucked away in the attic with her mother's things. The things inside it meant something. She just didn't know what.

She heaved a sigh as she turned to cross West Main in the usual place, walking on auto-pilot, because she knew the way by heart. She'd been walking it for a long time now. As she crossed, she glanced at the shop across the street. *Gwenyth's Chamber.* She'd been in there a few times, even picked up a couple of books. But when she'd worked up the courage to ask the owner a few, tentative questions, the little blond had given her a sad smile and told her to come back when she was eighteen.

How was she supposed to understand what was happening to her if no one would even discuss it?

As she watched, Officer Cantone walked into the shop, and a second later, a woman walked out. Rowan frowned and looked closer. That was Miss Saint-A, her homeroom teacher! Coming out of that kind of a shop? But . . . did that mean that she . . . .

Before she could complete the thought, Miss St. A looked right at her, shouted something, and raced toward her. Startled, Rowan yanked off her headphones and glanced to her left. At first she saw nothing, but in a split second a truck careened around the sharp curve and was bearing down on her. And for just an instant she was frozen in panic.

Then Miss Saint A's body crashed into hers, and the impact hurled her out of the way. The two of them hit the pavement together in one big tangle. The landing hurt like hell–and Rowan had landed on top!

# # #

Bella wasn't sure what happened. She came out of Gwenyth's shop and looked up to see a woman.

And then she froze, because it was the same women she'd glimpsed in her bathroom mirror this morning!

The woman lifted a hand and pointed.

"Who are you? What the hell do you want with me?"

But the woman shook her head harshly and jabbed her finger again and again toward the road. Bella turned to look, she saw the girl in the road, and in a flash, she knew the truck was coming. Before she saw it, before she heard it, she *knew* it. She shouted a warning and ran.

The truck came thundering then, and the girl seemed frozen in fear. Bella's body crashed into hers, and her momentum carried them both to the roadside, to the pavement, hitting hard. The girl's breath burst from her lungs with an "unh!" when they landed.

Tires squealed and Bella smelled burning rubber even before she turned to see the smoke rolling off the wheels as the truck came to a stop a block down, cockeyed in the road.

She got to her feet, helping the girl up as well. For the first time, she realized it was one of her own students. Rowan Hawthorne.

Rowan was fourteen, brilliant, but moody. Often introspective and always questioning authority. Bella liked her. She brushed the dust from the girl's vinyl jacket and looked her up and down. "Are you all right, Rowan?"

Rowan nodded, looking dazedly at the truck, then back at Bella again. "That jerk almost killed me," she said, straightening her skirt with an angry tug. Then she glanced at Bella more closely, her eyes narrowing. "Your lip is bleeding, Miss Saint A. Are you all right?"

"I'm fine." She touched her lip, drew her fingers away, looked at the blood.

But Rowan's eyes were even narrower now. "God, look at your head."

Bella touched the spot where her head hurt, sucked in a breath and drew her fingers away. A lump seemed to be forming already, and it hurt like hell. People were coming toward them now from the shops on either side of the street.

"I didn't see that truck," Rowan said. "You yelled, and then he was just there. How did you know?"

"My God, my God, Rowan! Are you two all right?" The deep, male voice was accompanied by pounding footfalls as a man raced toward them.

Even as Rowan called "I'm fine, Dad," Mirabella turned to look his way. And the moment she saw his face, her blood rushed to her feet so fast she felt dizzy. Her vision swam, and she pressed a hand to her forehead automatically and closed her eyes.

He was beside them in a heartbeat, grabbing hold of her shoulders. "Hold on. Easy now, I've got you."

Gentle hands eased her down onto the sidewalk. Tender fingers pushed her hair aside. "Ah, you've got a nasty bump here. Maybe a slight concussion."

"I'm sure it's nothing like that." She opened her eyes again, hoping with everything in her that it had been a trick or a hallucination–that he would look totally different now.

But her wish was not granted. He was hunkering near her, his hands on her face, his eyes filled with concern and questions, not hate and rage. But he was the same. Dark hair, dark eyes. A face as hard and square as if it were a bust carved in marble.

The man from her dream.

And that meant the girl whose death Mirabella had some-how caused–had to be Rowan.

Bella looked at her. Young and stunningly beautiful, sit-ting beside her looking worried. Suicide. God, no. The very thought made Bella's eyes fill with tears.

"She saved my life, Dad. Did you see it?"

"I saw," he said, and he frowned just a little at his daugh-ter and reached out to pick up the fallen headphones. "Maybe these ought to come off when you're crossing streets, hmm?"

She shrugged sheepishly, and he smiled, then pulled her close for a gentle hug. "Are you sure you're okay, hon? God, if anything ever happened to you, I think I'd lose my mind."

"Dad, you're so melodramatic," Rowan said, but she hugged him back.

When he released her, he turned to Bella again. "Let me take you to the clinic, have that bump looked at."

Several of Bella's colleagues were gathered around them now, and Gwenyth and Officer Billy Cantone were coming to-ward them. Almost all the teachers who lived in town walked this route to school. Often they would meet in Granny Kate's Coffee Shop, a few doors away from Gwenyth's place, for a fresh baked doughnut and a hot mug of brew before heading in to work. No one in town was quite as well loved as Granny Kate.

"I'm fine, really," Bella said. She sought Gwenyth's eyes and repeated it. "Just a close call. I'm really okay." Gwen nod-ded, licking her lips and backing off. Bella knew she was trying to protect her. With so many colleagues around she didn't want to publicize their friendship. Officer Billy was already heading away to talk to the truck driver.

Bella started to get up to prove she was okay, only to have the man clasp her shoulders in his big hands and help her to her feet. "That bump doesn't look like something to be ignored," he said. His voice did things to her. She felt its reverberations echoing in her belly and in her throat.

"I really have to get to school." Did she sound a little breathless? He was standing too close, and his hands were still on her shoulders, and his eyes were all over her.

"School?" His brows rose, thick dark arches. "You're one of Rowan's teachers, aren't you?"

She nodded. "Mirabella Saint Angeline, Freshman English," she said.

"It's Miss Saint A, Dad. I've told you about her before." Rowan looked curiously from one of them to the other.

He nodded, not taking his eyes off Mirabella. "Odd, I was just thinking of you this morning." And when she only frowned at him in confusion, he said, "I'm Jonathon," he said. "Jonathon Hawthorne. Rowan's father."

That much, she'd gathered on her own.

"I really think you ought to let Dad take you to that clinic, Miss Saint A," Rowan said. "You don't look too good. And I feel guilty enough already."

"You shouldn't feel guilty at all, Rowan."

"I won't–once I know for sure you didn't give yourself brain damage knocking me out from in front of that truck."

Mirabella lowered her head. Tough to argue with that.

Someone reached out to hand Mirabella her soft sided briefcase. Bella followed the hand up the arm to see who was attached to the other end. Sally Hayes, the high school principal. Salt and pepper hair and a designer suit. No mistake. Bella lifted her brows. "What are you doing here, Sally?"

"I was driving by and saw the crowd. I agree with them both, Mirabella," she said, nodding toward Jonathon Hawthorne and his daughter. "Go get yourself checked out. I insist. I'll handle your classes myself today if we can't get a sub."

There was an odd look on her face, though. A speculative look, and as Bella took her case from the woman she thought she realized why. A paper bag was clearly visible, sticking up from a side pouch on the case. The logo on the bag was a Witch on a broomstick in black silhouette, and the words "Gwenyth's Chamber" were stamped across the top.

She'd picked up a few supplies while visiting Gwen this morning. But she'd put the bag in the center portion of the briefcase, and she thought she'd zipped it. Apparently, though she hadn't. Somehow it must have fallen free during the near miss, and Sally Hayes had tucked it back into the briefcase.

Which could mean she knew what was in it.

Nothing all that incriminating, really. A handful of altar candles in various colors, some patchouli oil, and a plastic zipper bag full of Gwenyth's homegrown rue. It shouldn't make Bella feel suddenly nervous or worried. But it did.

"Now you see?" the man was asking. "Everyone agrees you should be looked at. And besides, you just saved my daughter's life. It's the least I can do."

Reluctantly, knowing full well she shouldn't, Mirabella nodded. "All right." Frankly, she just wanted to be out of the spotlight as soon as possible. She didn't like all these people milling around looking at her. It was too much like the dream.

"Good." Jonathon Hawthorne turned to his daughter. "Maybe you'd better be checked out too. What do you think?"

"I didn't even get a scraped knee, Dad," Rowan said. "Miss Saint A landed on the pavement, and I landed on top of her. I'm fine. But I'll go see the school nurse before first period if you want."

"You do that." He sent the principal a glance.

"I'll make sure she does," Sally Hayes said. Then she smiled at Mirabella. "You're a hero today, Mirabella. Take the whole day off, if you like. And let me know if you need more time."

"Thank you," Bella said.

"Come along, Rowan. You can walk the rest of the way to school with me."

Rowan averted her face from the principal's view before she rolled her eyes. "Dad's going to drop me off, Mrs. Hayes. It's on the way to the clinic."

"Oh. All right then," Sally said.

Rowan's father turned Bella around, one hand on her arm, as if he thought she might fall again at any moment, and led her and his daughter across the street. His shiny black car stood cockeyed where he'd apparently skidded to a halt in panic at seeing his daughter nearly flattened by a truck. He opened the front passenger door, took Bella's briefcase from her, and held it as she got in. Then he leaned in, fastened her seatbelt for her, and handed the case back to her.

Bella shoved the Gwenyth's Chamber bag deeper into the front pouch, out of sight.

Rowan got into the back seat, and a second later, her father was behind the wheel and pulling away.

Chapter Three

He drove, she rode, and neither of them spoke much once they'd dropped Rowan at school. But he kept finding his gaze drawn to her, and since she mostly stared out the window, it was easy enough to look his fill. He wasn't sure what there was about the woman that should send warm waves pleasure surging through his insides every time he touched her or looked too deeply into her eyes. Probably no more than the fact that he'd just seen her save his daughter's life, and his daughter was everything to him.

Yeah. That was all it was.

Her hair wasn't all that striking—even though it was the blue black of a raven's wing. And her eyes were *not* that enticing—just because their marbled green color was so vivid. Like malachite. Probably colored contacts, he imagined. And her shape was nothing to get this worked up about. Sure she was willowy, leggy, lithe. But so were a lot of women these days. It wasn't that unusual.

The only thing different about her was her heroism in the face of a speeding truck. And the dirty smudges on her proper pearl-colored skirt and matching blazer. The run in her nylons. The bruise on her pretty cheek where she'd come between his precious Rowan and the pavement.

Yeah. No wonder she looked good to him. It wasn't attraction. It couldn't be attraction, because he didn't *do* attraction. Hadn't been drawn to another woman since Ashley died.

"I . . . um. . . . can get someone to bring my car to the clinic. You can just drop me and go on your way. I don't want to make you late for work," she said, when she turned and caught him staring.

"I think the DA's office will survive the morning without

me."

She went a little stiffer, and he saw her eyes flare just slightly wider. "You're a prosecutor?"

"Not nearly as exciting as it sounds. Ezra Township is pretty much typical of the entire district. Rural. Quiet. We don't see a lot of crime out here. At least . . . not until recently."

He parked the car, got out, and she did too, even before he could get around it to open her door. He walked close to her, in case she had another dizzy spell or stumbled. Or . . . that was why he told himself he was walking so close. She shivered when his arm brushed hers, and he wondered why. Was she feeling this odd attraction as well?

"Are you talking about the animal mutilations, Mr. Hawthorne?"

"Disgusting, isn't it?" He sighed and shook his head.

They stopped outside the door of the clinic, and she turned, looked up at him. "Do you think the police have any idea who's behind them?"

"I'm sure they do. But um . . . I can't really discuss it beyond that."

"Of course not."

He opened the door, held it for her, and she went inside. He stood back while she checked in at the receptionist's desk. Then she came back to him. "It's a slow day," she said. "They can get me right in."

"Great. I'll be waiting."

She bit her lower lip, worrying it with her teeth in a way that made his stomach clench up. He said, "Unless . . . you're not comfortable with me sticking around a bit longer. I only want to be sure you're all right."

"No, I . . . No. It's fine."

She *was* uncomfortable with him. He could tell. It made him wonder why. Made him want to find out. He supposed that was in his nature. His role at work lent itself to a good deal of investigating. Leg work. Some of the lawyers in the office pre-ferred to hire investigators. He preferred to do it himself.

He sat down, picked up a magazine and watched her disappear through the door and into the exam room. A half-hour later she came out again, and the only real difference he saw was that she'd washed the smudges off her face. Dr. Plummer came out behind her, a chart in her hand. She was the stereotype of a small town doctor in every way except gender. She was aging, white haired, kindly, and brilliant.

Jonathon got to his feet. "Well?"

"I'll live," Mirabella said with a nervous little smile.

The doctor looked up from the chart. "She probably has a slight concussion, but that's not serious."

"Then . . . she should be in a hospital, shouldn't she?" Mirabella sent him a quick frown, but he pretended not to notice.

"Not necessarily," Dr. Plummer said. She just needs watching for the next twenty-four hours. Any vomiting, fainting, severe dizziness, just call me. I don't think there will be."

He licked his lips, sent Mirabella a silent look. She sent one right back, telling him to keep his mouth shut. He did, but he didn't like it. She hitched her purse up higher on her shoulder, thanked the doctor with a smile, and headed out of the clinic. Jonathon really had no choice but to follow.

He waited unto they were back in the car, no longer. "So how are you going to be watched closely for twenty-four hours if you live alone?"

She swung her dark eyes right up to meet his. "How do you know I live alone?"

"Well, I . . . I mean, I assumed . . . " He frowned. Since when did he stammer around a female? "It is *Miss* Saint Angeline, isn't it?"

She shrugged. "Sure. But I could live with someone."

"Do you?"

She averted her eyes. "No, but that's beside the point."

"Actually, it's not." He sighed. "So where do you live? I'll drive you home."

"I'm not going home. I'm going to school."

He braced his hands on the wheel, turned to look her dead in the eye and said, "Please don't."

She blinked as if in surprise.

"Look, I'm way out of practice at this knight in shining armor routine. And if I take you to work, and you keel over halfway through the day, it's gonna ruin the entire effort. *And make me look really bad to my daughter.*"

Her expression softened a little. He thought she might have almost smiled. "She means a lot to you, your daughter."

"Rowan is all I have in the world."

She frowned, tilted her head to one side. "I think your wife would disagree with that."

"My wife died ten years ago."

"I'm so sorry," she said. "I . . . didn't realize . . . ."

"Look, the point is, you are my daughter's favorite teacher. And I had every intention of calling you today anyway. And now you've gone and hurt yourself protecting Rowan from a runaway truck, and you don't even want to let me see you home. Put yourself in my shoes for a minute, will you?"

She looked at him oddly, as if she suspected him of some dire ulterior motive. But softly, she said, "All right. You can take me home. It's out on Sycamore."

"That's only a few blocks from us. We're on Highland." He smiled and put the car in gear, pulled out of the parking lot and headed toward her house.

"And on the way," she said, "maybe you can tell me why you were planning to call me today."

"Right." He took a breath, chose his words with care. The last thing he wanted was to say anything that seemed negative about his daughter. She was brilliant, and deep, and thoughtful and wonderful. "I wanted to talk about Rowan." He glanced sideways at her, watching her reactions.

A quick frown bent her brows and she looked at him intently, all defenses, all wariness gone. He liked that, that swift, concerned reaction. "Why? Is something wrong?"

"I was hoping you could tell me."

# # #

He dropped her off at her home, insisted on walking her to the door, and left his card with his beeper and cell phone numbers on the back for her to use in case she needed anything.

She went inside, closed the door, and watched him until his car was out of sight. Then she snatched up the phone and called Gwenyth.

"I know who he is!" she all but shouted when her best friend picked up.

"What? Who? Bella, what are you talking about?"

"The man. In the dream! I know who he is. His name is Jonathon Hawthorne and he's a prosecutor for the district attorney's office. His daughter is a student of mine. Rowan."

She could almost see Gwen's frown. "Is this the girl you pushed out of the path of that truck this morning?"

"Yes!"

"And that was her father you drove away with?"

"Yes!"

"Are you freaking out of your mind, Mirabella?"

"Yes! No. I don't know." Bella pushed a hand through her hair and paced the room. "He said he was going to call me anyway today. To talk to me about Rowan. He says she's been going through some drastic changes, lately, and he's worried about her."

"What is she, thirteen, fourteen?"

"Fourteen."

"And he's worried about changes?" Gwenyth blew a sigh. "Fourteen-year-olds are made up of changes. If you cut them open, changes are what you see writhing around in their insides. What is he, from Mars or something?"

Bella paced the floor, licking her lips. "No, there's more to it. He was holding a lot back, I could tell. But he was talking to me about her . . . he says she's starting to show interest in the Craft–or, the 'occult' as he calls it. She's been asking questions that make him uncomfortable. And he seems determined to put a stop to it."

"Do you blame him? The only things he probably knows– thinks he knows–about the Craft are butchered kitties and de- faced tombstones." She sighed. "Why doesn't he have Rowan's mother talk to her? I mean, women tend to understand these things . . . ."

"She's dead. Died ten years ago, he said."

"Oh. Oh."

"I don't know what to do here, Gwenyth. I mean . . . if I talk to Rowan about the Craft–"

"You can't do that! Good grief, after that dream? Are you insane?"

"But in the dream the girl committed suicide! If she knew the truth about things, that never would have happened. Maybe it was because I didn't get to her soon enough. Maybe she's going to get involved with this group of phony wanna-bees who go around murdering animals. Maybe my telling her would–"

"He's a prosecutor. You saw a vision that was supposed to warn you away from this pair, not send you straight to the stake!"

"That part was symbolic and you know it."

Gwenyth sniffed indignantly. "You hope."

Mirabella sighed. "I'm going to go meditate on this for awhile. I'll call you later, okay?"

"Sure. Later. In the meantime, though, hon, be careful. Watch your back. I mean it."

"I will." With a sigh she hung up the phone.

Several hours later, Bella's doorbell chimed.

Mirabella turned toward it, only to see Rowan Hawthorne standing on the other side, looking in at her.

Chapter Four

Jonathon sat in on the unofficial questioning of Bryan Marcomb. Bryan was seventeen, all limbs, with dark greasy hair and a goatee he must have thought looked cool. His mother had brought him in at the police department's request. He had a lawyer with him, but not a very good one. The guy was dead silent throughout the interview.

"You understand, you're not being charged with anything yet," Officer Cantone said. "But you *were* seen running away from that cemetery the other night. We know you were there." The final line was delivered with a grimness that let the kid know he was in trouble. Cantone was a good guy–his only faults, so far as Jonathon could tell, were a beer belly and a lack of tolerance for the foolishness of youth.

The kid rolled his eyes.

Cantone narrowed his. "The only reason we haven't charged you yet is because we haven't decided what to charge you *with*." The kid's eyes widened just a little. "What, you're surprised by that?" the officer asked him. "You thought we brought you down here to play patty-cake? All I wanna know is this—did you participate in whatever sick little party was going on out there that night? Or were you just a spectator?"

The kid lowered his gaze and pressed his lips together. His harried looking, dough-faced mother gripped his arm and squeezed. "Answer the policeman, Bryan."

With a sigh, Bryan looked up at Cantone again. "I was just hanging out."

"Then why did you run?" the cop asked.

He shrugged. "Why'd you chase me? When someone chases me, I tend to run."

Cantone's sigh should have sent papers flying off desks. "Look, you couldn't have been there and not seen something. So either you tell me what it is, or I have to assume you're a part of it! Got that?"

No reaction. The cop looked at the mother. "I thought you said he'd cooperate."

"She don't speak for me," Bryan spat. "I don't know anything. I'm not saying anything."

For just a second there was something in the kid's eyes. Something that made Jonathon frown and look closer. It had been brief, that flash. But for just a second, the kid had looked afraid. Truly afraid.

Almost as afraid as Mirabella Saint Angeline had looked when she'd first seen him this morning, Jonathon thought. And then he wondered how she was doing and thought about giving her a call. The woman had been haunting his thoughts all day. He could get lost in her eyes, even when he only saw them in his mind. What the hell was it about her?

He forced his mind back to the task at hand, back to the kid.

"Have you ever been inside a shop called Gwenyth's Chamber, Bryan?" Officer Cantone asked.

"That Witch shop in town, you mean? Sure, I've been in

there. She has cool stuff. What's that got to do with anything?"

"Just let me ask the questions, here, all right? What kind of cool stuff does she have that interests you?"

"I don't know, just stuff."

"Do you know the owner?"

Bryan frowned. "The blonde who runs the place? Not really." Bryan looked at his mother. "Can we just go now? Please?"

Mrs. Marcomb pursed her lips, looking mad as hell. But Jonathon thought it was more worry for her son than real anger. She loved the kid, though he was probably driving her nuts.

"You can go," Jonathon said. When Officer Cantone opened his mouth to object, Jonathon shot him a silent message. The cop read it, and nodded, and the mother and son hurried out of there.

"He was there," Cantone said.

"Yeah, but he's not fooling anyone with that tough-boy routine. I don't know if he's a part of this or not, but I do know he thinks he's in serious trouble if he talks to us. He was scared, Billy."

"So what do you suggest we do?" Cantone asked.

"I think you gave him a lot to think about here. Let's give him a few days. I have a feeling he'll be back."

Pursing his lips, the cop nodded. "Okay, we'll try it your way."

Jonathon left and hurried down the hall to his own office in the small, two-story County Building in Branwich, biggest town in the district, which was still a small town by most standards. It boasted a Wal-Mart, a handful of grocery and drug stores, one movie theater and two video rental places. Ezra Township was fourteen miles away.

He closed his office door, picked up the phone, and punched in Mirabella Saint Angeline's number . . . which, for some reason, he'd already committed to memory. Probably from having almost dialed it at least ten times today. He supposed it was natural to want to check in, make sure she was all right. Hell, she was all alone out there in her little cobblestone cottage with its vine covered walls and its big front porch. He didn't think he'd ever seen so many sets of windchimes in one place before.

Her telephone rang three times. He was about to hang up and head over there to check in person, when she picked up on the fourth ring.

"Hello?"

"Mirabella?"

Bella heard him say her name, and she shivered down deep in reaction to it. It wasn't just out of fear, either. There was something deeper. Something primal that experienced the sound of his voice like a physical touch.

It occurred to her that it was the first time he'd called her by her first name. And for some insane reason, she responded the same way.

"Jonathon," she said, when she could catch her breath. "I'm . . . surprised to hear from you." It was a lie. She'd been all but staring at the phone waiting for his call today. She lifted her gaze as she spoke, to watch his daughter, pacing in the next room. Mirabella had only just let her in when the telephone had interrupted them.

"I thought I'd check in. Just to, you know, make sure everything's still okay."

"Everything's fine."

"No dizzy spells or anything?"

"Not a one."

"Good."

He went silent for a long moment. She cleared her throat. "I . . . have company," she said. "So I really should–"

"Man or woman?" he asked.

She blinked in surprise at the bluntness of that question. But licking her lips she said, "Woman. Why?"

"Curiosity got the best of me, I guess. I, um . . . never mind."

"No. Tell me, what were you going to say?"

When he spoke again, his voice was much deeper, and a lot softer. "I haven't been able to stop thinking about you all day." He paused. "I know, that sounds like the world's worst pick up line. It wasn't."

"I know."

"Do you?" He cleared his throat uneasily. "Does that mean you feel there might be . . . something going on here. Between us?"

She closed her eyes, and her stomach knotted up. "There's something, Jonathon."

He sighed as if in relief. "I'm glad it's not just me. If you knew how unlike me this is, I . . . ." He stopped there. "You said you had company. I'll let you go."

"Thanks."

"But I'll call again later on."

She shook her head. "You don't need to."

"Actually, I think I do."

She frowned. "What's that supposed to mean?"

"Damned if I know. I'll talk to you later, okay?"

"Okay."

"Take it easy. Rest, like the doc said."

"I will. Good-bye, Jonathon."

"Bye."

She hung up the phone, stared at it for a moment, and wondered why her heart was fluttering wildly in her chest. Why the stroke of each tone of his voice against her eardrums had been an erotic experience. Why she was breathless by the time she said good bye.

She gathered her composure, bit by bit, and finally, lifted her chin, and walked back into the parlor where Rowan waited. "Sorry for the interruption. We can talk now. Please, sit down."

Rowan did, choosing the claw legged chair with the embroidered upholstery and looking like a nervous princess, taking her throne. The girl was nothing less than stunning. And her eyes could stop traffic.

"How's my dad?" she asked.

Miraballa blinked. "You were listening?"

"Only a little. Thanks for not telling him I was here."

"I didn't think he'd approve of you leaving school over an hour early any more than I do. Care to tell me why you did that?"

She shrugged. "I told Principal Hayes I was shaken up

and sore from the accident. But really I just wanted to come and see you."

"To make sure I was okay?" Mirabella asked.

Rowan lowered her eyes. "Partly that."

"Well, I'm okay. So we can go on to the other part."

The girl licked her lips, lifted her head slowly and stabbed Bella's eyes with her own. "Are you a Witch?"

Mirabella lifted her eyebrows and sucked in a breath. It took her a moment to formulate a reply, but she managed to find one. "That's a very personal question Rowan. Maybe a little bit too personal. May I ask what makes you want to know?"

"Because . . . you can do things. And I want to know what it means."

Bella waited, but Rowan stopped there. "Well, come on, Rowan. Don't leave me hanging. What kinds of things are you talking about?"

Biting her lower lip, Rowan got to her feet, paced to the middle of the
room and turned to face Mirabella. "You shouted that warning before the truck ever came into sight. You knew it was coming."

Lowering her head, Bella closed her eyes at the pealing of the warning bells in her mind. "How do you know I didn't just hear the truck coming?"

"Because I didn't hear it."

"You had your headphones on."

"I yanked them off. There was no sound–not until a second or two later."

Bella shook her head slowly and got to her feet. She didn't mention the woman she'd seen pointing frantically, because when she'd looked around for her in the moments after the near miss–she hadn't seen her. And she knew damn well that was because the woman wasn't someone physical. She was a spirit.

Bella said none of this to Rowan. Instead, she said, "Come with me. We need tea."

Rowan followed her into the kitchen, where Bella put on a kettle of water, and dug two antique metal tea balls from a drawer. She opened her cupboard, on rows of glass jars, each containing herbs most of which either she or Gwyneth had grown, dried, and ground themselves. As she dipped from one of the jars, she said, "This is my special, calming blend. Chamomile, valerian, a bit of lavender." She measured tea into each tea ball, then dropped them into a pair of china cups, leaving their chains dangling over the sides. Rowan took a seat at the small round table.

"So you think I sensed that truck coming before I could see or hear it?" Mirabella asked.

"Yes. I know you did."

"And that makes you think I might be a Witch?"

Rowan shook her head. "More than just that. I saw you coming out of that shop. Gwenyth's Chamber. And you bought stuff in there. It was in your briefcase."

"I like herbs. I make homemade teas. Does that make me a Witch then?" She was stalling, really. Fishing. She knew too well that Rowan was the girl in her dream. And she was scared to death of the idea that the child could die because of something Bella might teach her. Apparently, something about Witchcraft. She had to be extremely careful what she said to this child.

She heard the water start to boil and poured it into the cups. Then she carried them to the table, went to the fridge for cream, set out the sugar, and finally sat down and moved the teaball by its chain in slow circles in the cup, to calm her nerves.

"Rowan, why don't we chalk it up to women's intuition and call it good, hmm?" She sipped again. "After all, why should it matter what I am?" She took a sip of her tea, but it was still weak.

"Because I need to know what I am. Am I a Witch, Miss Saint A? Is there any way to tell?"

The tea sort of gushed backward up Bella's windpipe and out her nose.

Now that she'd started, though, Rowan rushed right on, speaking faster with every sentence and barely pausing for a breath in between. "The other day, someone called me a name in the hall at school, and I turned around, really angry, and when I did, the posters fell off the walls. All the way up the hall from where I was standing to where the other person was. It was a good ten feet. And I knew it was that rush of anger that knocked them all down. It was like I could feel it surging out of me, you know? And then last night, my dad got on my case for some stupid thing or other, and I went up to my room, spun around to slam the door, only it slammed itself, before I ever touched it." She set her tea down, got to her feet, and paced the room. "Miss Saint A, stuff like that happens to me all the time. More than just what could be coincidence or explained away. More than I can understand. Dad says it's all in my head, and to tell you the truth I was beginning to wonder if he was right. But then my mother started coming to me . . . in my dreams. And it's like she's trying to tell me something, and I don't know what it is, and–"

Tears seemed to choke her. They welled up in her eyes, and her voice got tighter until it tightened into silence.

Bella got up and went to her, clasped her shoulders, and looked right into her ocean blue eyes. "You're *not* crazy. There's nothing wrong or even all that unusual about what's happening to you, Rowan."

Rowan sniffled and brushed at her eyes. "Really?"

"I promise. I . . . . " Mirabella closed her eyes, bit her lip. Hell, she was risking her job and Jonathon's anger by even saying a little. But the girl was in pain. What choice did she have? Could she really just bite her tongue and watch this incredible young woman suffer?

No. She couldn't.

So she choose her words carefully. "I believe we all have more than the five senses we acknowledge. A lot of other people believe it too. Doctors, scientists, world leaders."

Blinking, searching her eyes, Rowan said, "What kinds of senses?"

Bella shrugged. "Oh, psychism, or telekinesis. Picking up on thoughts. Causing physical movement by the power of will and emotion. And there are lots of other extra senses we have too. Precognition . . . . "

"Like when I reach for the phone before it rings, and already know who's on the other end. Or hum a song and turn on the radio and hear it playing?"

"Yes. Just like that. It's pretty widely accepted by those

who study such things, that there are two times in life when these . . . other senses . . . are naturally strongest. One is when we're very young. Babies, toddlers. Before society has convinced us that such things don't exist. And the other time, is during puberty. Particularly in girls."

The relief that flooded Rowan's face made Mirabella know it was worth the risk. She'd said very little. And somehow, she had given Rowan something she'd desperately needed; validation, assurance that she wasn't losing her mind.

"You're not just saying this to make me feel better?"

"No. I'm not."

She smiled, though her tears were spilling over now. Down her cheeks. "Then. . . everyone has these powers? Not just . . . Witches?"

"Everyone has them to one degree or another. Witchcraft is just the name given to the art of mastering them, learning to control them, and make them stronger. Well–that's a part of it, anyway."

"And what's the rest of it?"

Mirabella lowered her eyes. "You haven't even tasted your tea."

Rowan returned to her seat, calmer now, and sipped the tea, then licked her lips and sipped it again. "It's good," she said. "Miss Saint A, what do you think my mom is trying to tell me?"

"I don't know. Maybe she's just letting you know she's still with you, watching over you," Mirabella mused, returning to her seat as well.

Rowan seemed to think on that for a moment. "I don't think that's it. She always seems . . . agitated. Worried about something. Her lips move like she's trying to say something, but I just can't hear her."

Frowning, Mirabella sensed the girl was not referring to a dream. Not an ordinary one, anyway.

Funny, how they'd both received messages during dream time, neither of which could be cast off as dreams. And how they seemed to be on a path that was determined to cross. "What was your mother's name, Rowan?"

"Ashley," she said, softly, wistfully. "Ashley Rowan

Hawthorne. And I'm Rowan Ashley."

There was a powerful mother-child bond at work here. She could feel it clearly. "How do you feel when she comes to you?" she asked, hoping to get some clue what the message might be.

Rowan closed her eyes. "First . . . it's just joy to see her. She's so beautiful. And so real. Dad says I look just like her. But I think he's exaggerating. Sometimes I wish I didn't have to wake up at all, just so I could still be with her."

A little bolt of alarm shot through Bella. "She wouldn't want that, Rowan—for you to leave this lifetime before you were meant to. She wouldn't want that at all."

Rowan studied her, tilting her head to one side. "I know that." Then, sighing deeply, she took a small pouch out of her pocket. "I found this in the trunk in the attic, where my dad keeps all my mom's things." Gently, she opened the pouch, and tipped it up so its contents spilled out onto the table. A handful of crystals–quartz, tiger's eye, amber and jet. Some rose petals. A seashell. A bit of hair, its color so deeply auburn it had to have been Rowan's own. The lock was fine, curling, baby hair, bound in a pink ribbon. There was a feather, raven or perhaps crow. And a silver five pointed star, enclosed with a circle, on a long chain.

"Does your father know you have this?"

"No. He wouldn't like it. Does it mean what I think it means? Was my mother . . . was she a Witch?" Rowan picked up the pentacle. "Isn't this an evil symbol?"

Bella closed her hand over Rowan's around the star, then turning it palm up, opened the girl's fingers. She traced the star with her own. "Earth," she said, tracing the point in the three o'clock position. "That's your body and your home." She traced another point. "Air, your mind and your breath." Tracing the next, she said, "Water, your blood and your emotions." And the next, "Fire, your energy and your passion." Finally, she moved her finger over the topmost point. "Spirit–the life force that lives in all of us.

"What most people call God or Goddess, is, to me, the Source from which we come, to which we return, and of which we are always a part. It's alive in each of us, and it's the sum total of us all. That's what the circle around the star means. That we're all connected. That's what your mother believed in, Rowan. That's why she wore this symbol. There's nothing evil about that."

Another tear, a relieved one, Bella thought, rolled slowly down Rowan's ivory cheek. She smiled, sniffed noisily. "Then she wasn't into murdering cats or anything like that?"

Bella was probably getting herself in too deep. But she had come this far. She didn't suppose she could make things much worse by giving the girl one more kernel of knowledge, to ease her mind. "There's one cardinal rule in the Craft of the Wise, Rowan. And that is to harm none. No true Witch would hurt another living thing."

Rowan looked up, eyes widening slowly. "You know so much about this . . . does that mean, you really are . . . ?"

"Yeah. I really am. But if it gets out, Rowan, especially with the stuff that's been going on in town lately, I could be in a lot of trouble. Not everyone understands. Not everyone wants to."

"I'm not going to say anything to anyone," Rowan promised.

"I don't want you to lie either. If you're asked, tell the truth. The thing is . . . by talking to you at all, I'm putting us both in an awkward position. I don't feel very good about discussing this stuff with you behind your father's back."

Rowan lowered her head. "I don't understand why he's so against it. I mean, he had to know about Mom."

"Maybe you need to talk to him. Openly and honestly. If you can get his permission, I'll help you learn to understand more about it all."

"But what if he says no?"

Mirabella lowered her eyes. "Then I'll give you suggestions for some good books on the subject, and . . . and then, I don't know. We'll see." Reaching out, she stroked the girl's hair. "I promise you, it's better to be honest with him from the start. You don't want to get into the habit of sneaking around, hiding things and lying to him. It can only lead to trouble."

She sighed heavily. Bella knew she disagreed. "Listen, whatever you do, no drastic measures, okay? I'm on your side. Please remember that. And when it comes down to it, so is your dad. No one loves you more than he does."

"I know that."

"So?"

She drew a breath, nodded as she blew it out again. "Okay. At least I know I'm not crazy."

"No. You just inherited a special gift from your mom. More than one, even." She nodded at the little empty pouch on the table. "That was your mother's power bag. Put the things back inside and keep it with you all the time. A lot of her energy lingers in those things. I felt it when I touched the pent. When you want to feel her near you, take them out, hold them. Wear the necklace if you want, under your blouse for now. But don't let anyone else handle them. You can add your own special treasures when they turn up, if you want to. Maybe hand it down to your own daughter one day."

Rowan looked at her for a second, then she reached across the table, slid her hand over Bella's, and squeezed it just once. "You don't know how much this talk means to me," she whispered. "Thank you, Miss Saint A."

"I think you may as well call me Bella, outside school, all right?" she said. Inexplicably, she felt tears brimming in her own eyes. "Now, do you need a ride home?"

"I've got the four wheeler."

"And a helmet, I hope?"

Rowan rolled her eyes. "You sound like my father."

Bella walked her through the house, to the front door, and watched her leave. Then she turned to head back to the kitchen to clean up the tea cups, but when she passed by the antique oval mirror in the hallway, she stopped in her tracks, jerked her head to the side, and stared wide eyed at her own reflection.

A pale skinned, auburn haired woman stood just behind her, but only for an instant. She met Bella's eyes with an intense, unreadable expression, then faded almost at once.

Dad says I look just like her...

Ashley, she thought. That's who the ghost was. She had

to be Ashley Hawthorne, Rowan's mother.

Jonathon's wife.

<u>Chapter Five</u>

By five-thirty, Jonathon had resisted calling her a half
dozen more times. But the temptation remained, even while he
drove the car home. So he postponed the inevitable by calling
Rowan first.

She snapped up the phone on ring number two, and her
"hello" was so cheerful that he held the phone away from his ear
and blinked at it in shock. Then he drew it back again. "Rowan?"
he asked.

"Hi, Dad. Are you on your way home?"

"Yeah, I am. You sound in a good mood. Should I take
that to mean you're fully recovered from your brush with disaster this morning?"

"Fully," she said. "I'm as good as new. I was a little
shaky, but then I talked to Miss Saint A this afternoon, and she—"

"She went in to school today?" he asked.

"No. Actually. . . ." She sighed.

"Actually?" he prompted.

"Miss Saint A. says I shouldn't get into the habit of keeping things from you, so here goes nothing. I went home early.
And I decided to go by her house to see how she was doing."

He was quiet for a moment. "Thank you for that," he
said softly.

"You're not mad?"

"No. Are you okay, hon? I thought you said you were
feeling better."

"Oh, I am. Now."

"Good. So how was she, when you saw her?"

"She was great, Dad. I mean, she wound up giving me
some herbal tea and making me feel better. Even though she's
the one who got banged up this morning."

He nodded slowly. "So it's safe to say she wasn't resting
when you got there."

"No. Not really. Dad . . . I was there when you called."

"Oh?" He tugged his tie loose and undid the top button of his shirt.

"I know you like her."

He licked his lips, shook his head at the phone. "I only just met her, Rowan."

"I know. She's like that. I mean, I liked her the first time I met her too, and I usually hate teachers on sight, even if I don't know them yet. There's something . . . special about Bella, though."

He lowered his head, gnawed his lip. His daughter was too perceptive for his own peace of mind.

"And I hate to think of her all alone in that big house making her own dinner tonight. I mean, after what she did this morning–"

"You want to invite her to dinner?" He battled a smile.

"Can we?"

"I guess. I don't know if she'll come, but–"

"Why don't you stop and ask her? It's on your way home anyway."

Yes, it was on his way home. He'd already been looking forward to driving by and trying to catch a glimpse of her as he passed. What was it about the woman. . . ?

"Dad?"

"What? Oh, yeah. It's on the way. I'll stop and deliver the invitation. Good idea, Rowan."

"I know it was," she said. "So I'll see you later, then?"

"Sure will. Love you, kiddo."

"You too, Dad."

"Rowan?"

"Hmm?"

He swallowed hard. "Thanks for being up front with me. You always can, you know. No matter what."

"It works both ways, Dad," she said.

He paused, sighed. "You're right. There is something . . . special about Bella."

"I know."

The phone clicked, and he folded his in half and tucked it

back into his pocket. Then he turned onto Sycamore, two blocks up, and into Mirabella Saint Angeline's gravel driveway. His feet crunched over the stones, tapped up the steps and across the porch, and then he rang the doorbell. He waited a few beats. No one answered. He tried listening for footsteps from within, but the place was far too noisy for that. She had at least a dozen sets of wind chimes out there, and beyond the tinkling of them, there were the birds. She had more birds flitting around than any other house on the block. Frowning, he rang the bell again, then peered through the glass. Odd.

He was just about to start imagining she'd had complications from that bump on the head and was lying unconscious somewhere inside, when he heard a sound from beyond the house— one loud enough to be heard above the din. The back yard? He trotted down off the porch and around back. And there she was, standing on a wobbly ladder, pouring bird seed into a feeder. Which, he supposed accounted for all the birds.

"Now that's what I call taking it easy," he remarked.

She jerked her head around, apparently startled. The ladder tipped. The bag of seed hit the ground with a thump, and Jonathon shot forward to prevent the lady from doing the same. The next thing he knew she was in his arms. She'd fallen, and he'd caught her, awkwardly. His arms were tight around her thighs, and his face was pressed to her abdomen . . . mostly. Her hands braced on his shoulders. A rush of desire rose up inside him like a sleeping dragon that had been poked with a sharp stick. It had been a long time since he'd been this close to a woman or held a feminine body this tightly to his. And in spite of his usually chivalrous nature, he took advantage. He lowered her slowly. His face slid over her belly, pushing her shirt up a little on the way. His five o'clock shadow rasped over her skin. He heard her catch her breath. To his credit he pulled back a little to let her breasts slide by his face without *quite* touching, but he held tightly enough so the rest of her was pressed to the rest of him all the way down, until her feet touched the ground.

His arms locked around her waist, her body flush against his and warm and soft, her face, only a breath away, there was just no stopping it. He kissed her. He didn't think about it first, and he didn't ask permission. He just bent his head and covered her mouth with his. Her lips parted on a soft sigh, and her arms curled around his neck. She kissed him back. Her tongue met his, stroked it, teased and tangled with it, and he trembled all over with heat and hunger and need.

God, it had been so long . . . .

Her kissed her for a long, long time. He picked her up off her feet again, and she wrapped her legs around him, hooked her ankles at his back. He cupped her head in one hand and her bottom in the other, and he fed from her lips like a man starving to death. And finally, he lifted his head just a little, and breathlessly, he said, "I don't know what this is . . . ."

"I don't either," she whispered.

"God, I want you. It doesn't make sense. It's too fast, too damn sudden, but . . . . "

"I know. I know, Jonathon. It's the same for me."

He kissed her again. Felt his own arousal pressed tight between her legs, and cursed the clothes they were wearing as he moved against her there.

She broke the kiss this time. Panting, breathless, her eyes heavy and passion-glazed, she whispered, "There are things you don't know about me, Jonathon. Things I have to tell you, before–"

The bleating sound of his telephone ringing cut her off. He stared into her eyes for a moment longer, while it rang again. He was out of breath, and his heart was thundering against her.

She untwined from him, put her feet on the ground, averted her eyes and said, "You'd better get it."

Nodding, never taking his eyes off her, he pulled the cell phone from his pocket, flipped it open, brought it to his ear.

"Daddy?"

It was Rowan. And the ragged sound of her voice jerked him roughly back into his right mind again. He blinked away the haze of passion or whatever the hell had been fogging his brain. "Rowan? Honey, what is it? What's wrong?"

Mirabella's face changed too, as she searched his with worry in her eyes.

"Oh, Dad, it's awful. I mean, I'm fine, but Shauna . . . ."

"Shauna Gordon?" he asked.

"It's awful, Dad. Just come home. Come home right now. Please?"

"I'm on my way." He wasn't even fully aware of gripping Mirabella's hand and pulling her along beside him until they were both in the car. He didn't think it had ever once occurred to her not to come along.

"What is it?" Bella asked. "Is she okay?"

"I think so. She said it wasn't her. It's something about her best friend."

"Yes, Shauna, I heard that much. She didn't say what?"

"No. Thank God we're so close."

# # #

Mirabella had been lost in his kiss, his touch, his very presence. But Rowan's phone call snapped her out of that in a hurry, and it was only moments before Jonathon was skidding to a stop in his own driveway.

It wasn't far from where her own house was, physically. Socially it was a world away. On his street, people lived in huge houses with paved driveways and swimming pools. The Hawthorne house was set apart from the others, around a curve in the narrow lane, and up a slight hill. It was bigger, fancier. Big brick fireplace chimney creeping up one side and floor to ceiling windows angling up all the way into the peak at the front. Cedar and glass. Welcoming rather than pretentious.

Jonathon cut the engine, and Mirabella drew a deep breath before getting out, wondering what was coming next. There was a distinct feeling of taking her life into her hands happening here. Not by rushing to Rowan's rescue at Jonathon's side. She couldn't help doing that. She wouldn't be who she was if she did any differently.

It was the dream. The warning. Someone was trying hard to warn her and Rowan. Mirabella wished to the heavens she knew why.

Jonathon opened the front door and clasped her hand again as he hurried into the house, through a foyer and living room that would have impressed anyone, into the smaller dining room beyond. That was where he stopped and just stood in the doorway, looking at his daughter.

Rowan was sitting on the floor, legs curled in front of her, phone to her ear, tear tracks streaking her pretty face. She looked up, met her father's eyes, and said, "My dad's here, Shauna. I'll call you back, okay? Will you be all right? Okay. No, really, only a few minutes. Promise. Bye." Rowan's lower lip trembled as she got to her feet. She dropped the cordless phone onto the table and met her father halfway across the room.

Jonathon folded her into his arms. "It's okay, baby. Whatever it is, it's all right. What happened to Shauna? Hmm?"

She shook her head against his chest. "Not Shauna, her boyfriend. He . . . God, I don't know if I can even say it. He hanged himself."

"Oh my God." Jonathon clutched her closer, his hand in her hair. "Honey, I'm so sorry. Was . . . was he a friend of yours, too?"

She gently extricated herself from her father's arms. "I knew him. We weren't close or anything, but . . . poor Shauna. She's so crushed over this. And I don't know what to say to her or how to make it better." She turned her gaze to Mirabella's then, sniffing and swiping at her eyes. "I'm so glad you're here."

"Of course I am, Rowan. As long as you need me." She opened her arms, and Rowan came and hugged her, too.

"Why would he do it, Bella?" Rowan asked. "Why would Bryan do something like this?"

Mirabella had been trying to put it together in her mind and hearing the boy's first name finally clicked it into place. Bryan Marcomb. A Junior in high school and a boy Mirabella knew as well as she knew any of the students. *God, what a waste.* "Mrs. Marcomb must be devastated," she said, stroking Rowan's hair.

She saw Jonathon's frown, saw the look he sent her.

"I should call her back. I'm so worried about her being alone right now. Not that she's *really* alone. I mean, her parents are there, and her sisters, but . . ." She turned to her father. "Maybe I should go spend the night with her, just to–"

"No." He said it so quickly Mirabella knew something was up. But he softened his tone immediately. "I think your friend needs time to work through this, and I think she should probably spend it with her family. Just for a day or so. Then you can be there for her too. Right now it . . . it's just too fresh."

His cell phone was jangling again. He reached down, shut it off without answering it. "Go ahead, honey. Call Shauna back."

Rowan sniffed and nodded. She reached for the cordless phone, then hesitated. "I don't know what to say to her."

"You're doing just the right thing," Mirabella told her. "Just talking to her and listening. It doesn't matter what you say, because there really isn't anything that can help ease the pain. What counts is you being there for her. So you talk and you listen for as long as she needs you to. And you feel good about being the kind of friend who comes through at times like this. Okay?"

She nodded. "Thanks, Bella."

"You're welcome. And when you finish listening to her talk it out, you can turn right around and talk it out for yourself. To me, or your dad, or both of us if you need to, for as long as you need to, until you feel better. Okay?"

She smiled just a little. "It's so sad."

"Yes it is. And totally senseless. Take note of that, Rowan. Take note of the incredible amount of pain Bryan's act has caused you, and Shauna, and his mother, his friends. And I promise you, it hasn't solved whatever problems he thought he had. Life is meant to be lived. To the natural end." She spoke faster, gripping the girl's shoulders for emphasis. "When you take that way out, you're only going to have to start all over from square one the next time around. It solves nothing. It changes nothing. It's a lifetime that has to be repeated. Know that, Rowan. *Really* know it."

Looking at her oddly, Rowan nodded. "I do know it. Bella, is anything wrong?"

Bella lowered her eyes, releasing the girl's shoulders, and drawing a steadying breath. "No. Go ahead and call Shauna. She needs you right now."

Nodding, Rowan dialed her friend back again. As she reached her and began talking, Jonathon took Mirabella's arm and led her back into the living room.

"What was all that about? That reaction? Do you have some notion Rowan might be a suicide risk?"

She swallowed hard. "He was in her peer group, even if just by extension, Jonathon. I was just . . . taking precautions."

He tipped his head to one side. "You haven't seen any symptoms of–"

"No. Honestly, I haven't seen a hint of depression in Rowan."

He searched her eyes, then nodded, and sighed in relief. "This is awful. I just saw that kid this morning."

"What kid?"

"Bryan Marcomb." His face was grim as turned to he pace the room.

"Why?"

"He was seen running from the cemetery the night of the most recent animal mutilation."

Bella frowned. "Jonathon, do you think he was involved?"

"I don't know. But I think he knew who was. And I got the distinct feeling he was afraid to talk about it." He lowered his head. "Dammit, I'd hate to think he was so afraid he chose suicide over talking to the police." Then he sighed. "Probably not. It was probably some twisted occult thing that pushed him over the edge."

Jonathon assumed that the boy had been involved in the Craft. And that it was responsible for his death. She shivered, because this was so close to her dream . . . a child, committing suicide, an adult blaming it on Witchcraft. She had the distinct feeling they'd just moved yet another step closer to the final disaster.

She wanted with everything in her to tell Jonathon the truth. To set the record straight, come clean with him. But it just wasn't the right time. Already he was turning his cell phone back on, hitting buttons. "That was my office before. No doubt calling to tell me about Marcomb's death." Then he paused in dialing, met her eyes, and offered a very slight smile. One hand rose to stroke her hair. "We have so much to talk about, you and I. I . . . I haven't felt this way in a very long time, Mirabella. I'm sorry all this had to come up now and get in the way."

"Rowan comes first," she told him. "And poor Bryan. You owe it to him to find out what's really going on. Go ahead. Make your calls."

Leaning in, he brushed her lips with his. "I was supposed to bring you home, make you a nice dinner, see to it you had a relaxing evening."

"Rowan's idea?"

"She thinks so."

"Make your calls," she said. "It smells like Rowan already started dinner. So while the two of you take care of this crisis, I'll go check on it. Okay?"

He nodded, drew one finger over her lips, and then sighing in regret, turned to finish dialing the phone.

Mirabella found her way to the kitchen on her own. But she felt cold inside despite the heat of the oven. She was on a runaway train, heading straight for disaster, and she was damned if she knew how to stop it in time.

Chapter Six

It was after ten by the time Bella finished helping Jonathon clean up from dinner and Rowan was settled into her bed, sleeping restlessly.

She sat beside him now, on a wicker love seat on the deck in back. Stars glittered by the thousands from a clear deep blue sky, and she wondered how death could lurk so near on such a beautiful night. The moon was nearly full, and it bore a rose colored halo this night. That gave Mirabella pause. Her mother used to call that a Witch Moon, because of the red garter the moon appeared to wear. In some traditions, the red garter was still a symbol of the Craft. Bella's mother always said a red ringed moon meant an added boost to a Witch's magickal powers. But others called that ruby halo "blood on the moon" and took it as a bad omen. A sign of danger.

Bella didn't know which belief was correct. Maybe both. Maybe the added danger made the boost of power necessary. Maybe that was why they came as one.

"You could stay, you know," Jonathon said softly.

She drew her gaze from the moon to look into his eyes.

"I didn't mean . . . . " He swallowed hard. "We have guest rooms."

She nodded. "If I stay I won't be in any guest room, Jonathon. And I think after what happened between us this afternoon, we both know it. Besides, I have some things I need to do tonight," she said, keeping her tone level with effort. It was difficult, out here, alone with him like this. She was finding herself more and more drawn to this man with every moment she spent near him. And that was dangerous. She knew it too well.

"Did I scare you off with that . . . that kiss?"

She lowered her head. "It was a little more than a kiss. If Rowan hadn't called, I . . . ." She lowered her head, licked her lips. In her mind she saw them tearing at each other's clothes in her back yard. Making love, standing up, in broad daylight. It had been that frantic, what had happened between them.

"I wish she hadn't called," he said, and his voice was coarse.

She lifted her head. His face was close. He bent to her, kissed her. And that heat began uncoiling inside her all over again.

He slid his mouth from hers, over her jaw, and to the tender skin of her neck. Bella tipped her head back and curled her fingers in his hair. His lips, his mouth and teeth on her skin . . . it was too good. Too wonderful to resist.

"I'll slow down if that's what you want." He murmured, lifting his head. His hand was at her blouse, his fingers fumbling with the buttons. "But tell me now." A button came loose. She didn't say anything. He undid another. And then his hand slipped inside her blouse, and inside her bra, and closed around her breast. His breath stuttered out of him as she sucked hers in at his touch. Callused skin. Warm and rough. "You're not saying anything," he whispered. He drew his thumb and forefinger together on her nipple.

So she said something. She said, "Do that again."

His smile was slow and deliciously devilish. He pinched again, harder this time, and she arched against him. He took her mouth, tugging the rest of the buttons free, and pushing the blouse aside. He took her bra off her, and bent to use his mouth where his hand had been. And it was such sweet torment to feel him suckling her, nipping and pulling as if he'd eat her alive.

He dropped to his knees, reading her mind, she thought. Her skirt afforded no defense at all. It was loose and he easily pushed it up and tugged her panties off. And then put his hands on her thighs and parted them. She watched him, looking at her. Liking what he saw. Touching her, parting and probing with his fingers. And then with a low moan, he opened her wide, and tasted her, and she thought she would lose her mind to the intensity of the feelings exploding inside her.

He pulled her to the deck with him, pulled her down on top of him, and he was inside her. Just that suddenly. They were one. Mirabella tipped her head back and rocked her body over his. And she knew in that instant just before she lost herself again to sensation, she knew that this was not simply sex. She was linked to this man. He would be her lover, or her executioner, her salvation or her ruin. Nothing in between.

She cried his name and fell against his chest. And he held her so gently, so lovingly.

"God, Mirabella, where the hell did you come from? How can this be?" he whispered into her hair. "How can it be?"

She kissed his neck, and his ear. "Our souls have danced before, Jonathon. And will again. What you feel right now is real. Hold onto it. Please."

Lifting her head slowly, she stared into his eyes, trying to see into his soul. "This. . . is real. Our souls know each other very well. But now . . . now we have to come back to the place we call reality the rest of the time. That place where you don't know me at all, and where you may not like me very much when you do."

"Not possible," he whispered. "Mirabella, I . . . ."

"Shhh." She pressed a finger to his lips. "We need to talk, Jonathon."

Gently, she kissed his mouth, and then she got off him, and slowly fixed her clothes, buttoned her blouse. He did likewise, though she could see he didn't want to. She sat on the wicker love seat, and he sat down beside her.

"Okay, mysterious Mirabella," he said, his tone loving, teasing. "What don't I know about you? You're beautiful. You're special. There's something about you that draws me like magic, Mirabella. And you love Rowan. A blind man could see that."

"It's true. I do love her. I'd risk my life for her."

He smiled at her, reaching out to straighten her hair. "I know that. You already have, as a matter of fact."

"And maybe I still am."

His brows bent until they touched. "What do you mean?"

She gave her head a rapid shake. "Will you tell me something, Jonathon?"

"Anything. Just ask."

She nodded. "Why do you hate anything having to do with Witchcraft so much?"

His face changed. The gentleness faded, and a hint of harshness came in its place. His jaw went tight, his eyes, narrow. "Why do you ask?"

Bella lifted both brows. "You said you'd tell me anything. So tell me this. Your wife was Witch, wasn't she?"

He sent her a swift, searching look, and for the first time she saw his eyes cloud with suspicion. "How do you know that?"

"Rowan told me."

His eyes went wider. "Then she knows?"

"Yes. She knows. And she knows you disapprove of it, and refuse to talk about it, and try to keep it secret from her."

"Wait a minute, wait a minute." He gave his head a shake. Bella . . . have you been talking to my daughter about . . . about *Witchcraft?*"

Bella swallowed hard. "Rowan asked me if her mother was the kind of person who went around butchering helpless animals and defacing tombstones with their blood."

He lowered his head slowly, pressing his palms to his forehead. "I didn't ask you what she talked about, Bella. I asked what you told her."

She drew a breath. "Well, what do you think I told her?" she asked. "I mean, for God's sake, Jonathon. Was she?"

"Was who, what?"

"Was your wife the kind of person who went around butchering–"

"No!" He shot to his feet as he said it, pacing slowly away. "No," he said more softly. "Ashley wouldn't even kill spiders."

Mirabella watched him and wished she didn't have to put him through this kind of pain, but she didn't have a choice. "What was it about her beliefs that you hated so much? I mean, there had to be something."

He shook his head. "I didn't know much about her beliefs. I didn't want to know." He met Bella's eyes. "And I still don't. It's a lot of ridiculous superstition, hocus-pocus bullshit that weakens minds, makes people believe in the impossible instead of focusing on hard, cold reality."

Bella frowned. "You really believe that?"

He nodded. "Of course I do. And it was my wife who proved it to me beyond any doubt."

Mirabella tilted her head to one side. "How?"

"She died, Bella." He sighed, pushing a hand through his hair. "She had ovarian cancer. She and her crazy friends thought they could beat it, even when the doctors had given up hope. But all their healing spells and chanting and herbal teas and candle burning didn't do a damn bit of good. If there were any such thing as magic or Witchcraft, then how could she have died? How could she possibly have been yanked away from me–from Rowan–so far before her time?"

Bella went to him, touched his face. "My sweet Jonathon . . . if it was before her time, she wouldn't have gone. She left because she had accomplished what she came into this lifetime to do. Maybe her mission was to give life to Rowan. Maybe she just wanted to experience being loved by a man like you. Or having a daughter, or . . . no one can say. But she's not really gone. She's only moved on."

He shook his head. "It's smoke and mirrors. Garbage. And now it's being used to twist young minds like that of Bryan Marcomb, and look at the results." He stared at her, shaking his head slowly. "You're a teacher, Mirabella. God, you of all people should know better than to believe in . . . in Witches, for God's sake."

"It would be awfully hard not to," she said. "Considering I am one."

He slammed his eyes closed, swore under his breath.

Mirabella took a step away from him. "I've kept the truth to myself long enough, Jonathon. Something's going on . . . something that involves you, and me, and Rowan. And . . . and maybe Ashley. Now you can believe what you want about me, my spirituality, my powers or lack thereof, but you must know damn well I would never do anything to hurt your daughter." She licked her lips. "She's in danger, Jonathon."

His head came up slowly, eyes narrowing on her. "What kind of danger?"

"The same kind that Bryan Marcomb was in."

"Suicide?" He gripped her wrists tight. "Suicide? For God's sake! What do you know? And how do you know it? Tell me, Mirabella."

She glanced downward, at where he held her, and he eased his grip, but didn't let go. "I don't know anything. Except that someone is trying to help me protect Rowan. When that truck almost hit her, I saw a woman, pointing, and I knew what was about to happen."

He frowned. "What . . . could the truck possibly have to do with–"

"Not the truck. The woman. She was . . . I think she was Ashley."

He released her wrists as if they'd turned into snakes and would bite him. His lips parted, and his face twisted into a grimace as if he'd just bitten into something sour. "My God. You're right, Mirabella. I don't know you. Not in the least."

She managed not to flinch at his words. She had to get through this, tell him everything. "I've seen her again, too. At my house, standing behind me in the mirror. And Rowan's been seeing her as well."

"Oh for the love of Christ!" He threw up his hands. "Enough. It's enough. Just stop it."

"She's trying to warn us. Dammit, she'd probably come to you too, if you weren't too closed-minded to let her."

"It's bullshit!"

"Is it?" She drew a breath, sighed deeply. Then lowering her head, shook it from side to side. "I guess it's time I went home." When he started to move, she held up a hand. "No. I'll walk. It's only a few blocks, and . . . I like the night."

"You shouldn't walk alone."

"I want to. I have a lot of thinking to do. And Jonathon, so do you. Rowan is hurting and confused. Maybe it would be a good idea for you to learn a little bit about what it is you're condemning before you write it off, hmm? For her sake? You don't have to agree with it. You don't have to believe in it. Just respect it for what it is, and know it for what it isn't. Witches don't sacrifice animals, Jonathon. And they don't drive kids to suicide."

He lowered his head. "I know that much."

"Do you? Do you really?" She shook her head slowly, and walked away.

"Bella?"

She turned slowly, looked back at him.

"Why the hell didn't you tell me this before you let me . . . . ."

"Let you what? Fall in love with me?" she said. Her voice was soft with unshed tears, but she knew he could hear her. "We've been in love for a long, long time, Jonathon. Before we ever met, I think." She lowered her head. "But you don't believe in that kind of thing, do you?"

Turning, she walked away.

# # #

There was a pall over the entire town as she walked through it to school the next morning. But she stopped, when she saw the bright red spray paint and the broken glass at Gwenyth's place. Across the front wall, in bloody lettering, were the words, "Suffer not a Witch to live."

"Oh no," Bella whispered as a cold hand closed around her heart. "Oh, Goddess, please, no!" Racing across the street toward the shop with her heart in her throat, she shouted, "Gwen! Gwenyth!"

Gwen came out the door before she even got there. "Oh,

thank goodness!" Bella said, grabbing Gwen and hugging her hard, kissing her cheek. "Thank goodness. Are you okay? Hmm?" She backed off, pressing her palms to the sides of Gwen's face. Her cheeks were tear streaked and her eyes, puffy. But she was in one piece, thank the Goddess!

Bella hugged her hard, looking past her at the men in overalls who were chipping the jagged pieces of glass out of the window, preparing to install a new one. Others were just arriving in a pick up truck, and unloading their paint and brushes. "Honey, what happened?"

"Circe's missing," she said, her voice raspy. "I'm so afraid they took her, and I just keep thinking about what's been going on with . . . with animals around here lately."

"Oh no," Bella whispered. "Come on, come inside, tell me everything." She kept one arm firmly around Gwen's shoulders as she led her into the shop, through it, and to the small parlor off the back that divided the shop from the rest of the house and served as Gwen's temple room. "Sit," Bella said, pressing her into a chair. "Now talk."

Gwen tugged a tissue from her pocket and swiped at her face. "It must've been around three a.m.. I heard the glass breaking. I came downstairs. The window was smashed, there was a brick on the floor." She shook her head slowly. "And I couldn't find Circe, so I went outside, calling, her and that's when I saw the paint on the front wall." She shuddered with her whole body at the memory. "I thought it was blood at first . . . ."

"Did you call the police?"

"Yes. They're calling it vandalism."

Bella frowned. "Vandalism? This is a hate crime!"

Gwen frowned, shaking her head slowly. "This is it, Bella. I can't take it anymore. I think I'm going to go ahead and take Mark Hayes' offer on the house."

"But you can't. This was your great-grandmother's legacy. Oh, Gwenyth, please think this over some more."

Gwen lowered her head.

"Look, at least don't make any decisions right now. Not when you're still this upset."

She sniffled, nodded. "I'm not going anywhere until I

find out what happened to Circe, at least."

"I'm sure she just got scared by the noise and ran off to hide. She'll show up soon." She reached across the table to clasp Gwen's hands. "You want me to make you some tea?"

"No. I'm fine, really. You . . . probably need to go."

Bella glanced at her watch. "I have another minute or two."

"Liar," Gwen said, dashing her eyes dry. "So how are things going with the prosecutor and his daughter?"

Bella pursed her lips and shook her head. "Well, his first wife was a Witch. He seems to think that because she died of ovarian cancer, that's some kind of proof that the entire belief system is bogus. And, he knows that includes me."

"You told him?" Gwen asked, wide eyed.

"I had to." She shook her head. "His wife's name was Ashley. And I'm pretty sure I've had a couple of visitations from her. So has Rowan."

Gwenyth lifted her brows. "She trying to drive you away?"

"No. I don't think so. She's trying to help me protect Rowan from . . . whatever the hell is about to happen to her."

"Then you have an ally."

"A powerful one, I think," Bella said.

Gwenyth smiled. "Well, if you see Witch Ashley again, would you ask her to look out for Circe, maybe send her home if she sees her?"

"Maybe you'll be able to ask her yourself. If you're up to a full blown ritual."

Gwen lifted her brows. "You want to try to stir her spirit, see if we can get some answers?"

"Yeah, and I'm thinking it might take the full coven to do it."

"We should have been working on uncovering the truth behind what's been going on in this town before now," Gwen said. "But everyone's been too damned scared of being found out to come to circle." She nodded. "But they'll come now. When and where, hon?"

"Tonight. The full moon's in Saturn. Couldn't be much

better timing." Bella frowned. "Are you *sure* you're up to this?"

"You bet I am." Gwen tried a shaky smile. "In fact, it's good to have something to focus on besides worrying about my precious feline. Go on, now, you'd better get to work before they fire you."

If only Bella had known how prophetic Gwen's parting words had been.

Chapter Seven

Mirabella walked into the school building, and knew immediately the place was deserted. Of students at least. An empty school had a feel to it that was different from anything else. Even a *nearly* empty one tended to exude a lonely, haunted feeling.

"Ms. St. Angeline?"

Mirabella turned her head sharply at the echoing voice and saw Sally Hayes standing in the open doorway of her office.

"Would you come into my office please?"

The woman turned before Mirabella could even answer, stepping back into her office, leaving the door open, leaving Bella no doubt she had just been summoned. A tiny shiver wandered up her spine. She knew beyond any doubt that this was not good.

Standing just inside the office doorway, she said, "Where are all the students?"

"We decided to cancel classes for today, Sally said. "Because of Bryan Marcomb's death. We felt the kids would need a day to deal with the shock. Tomorrow we'll have counselors on hand to help them talk through it."

Bella frowned. She hadn't had the TV or radio on this morning, so she hadn't heard the announcement that school was canceled. But she should have heard it, anyway. Staff were supposed to be notified by phone. "No one called," she said. "What happened to the telephone tree? Someone cut it down?"

"We didn't call you because we wanted to meet with you this morning, Ms. Saint Angeline."

Bella frowned at the cool, formal tone. "Since when did we stop being on a first name basis, Sally?" Then she looked past her at the closed door to the meeting room, just off this one. "And what do you mean, 'we'?"

Sally Hayes opened the meeting room door. "The school board," she said.

Beyond the door, Mirabella saw the members of the school board seated around a rectangular table. She knew these people. But she'd never feared them. Today they wore the grim, stony faces of a Puritan tribunal, and she felt more than a little bit afraid.

Frowning and fighting the chill that raced up her spine, Bella went inside. Sally Hayes came behind her, closing the door. "I think you know everyone," she said. "Please, have a seat." She indicated one of the two empty chairs at the table. She took the other, at the table's head.

Mirabella sat down. "Fine. I'll play. What's this all about?"

"Ms. St. Angeline, we have reason to believe that you are involved in the practice of the occult."

"What?"

"This emergency meeting of the board has been called in order to give you the chance to defend yourself against these accusations, and so that we may decide what action we need to take for the best interests of the students."

Bella looked slowly around the table. Not one of those present had the gumption to look her in the eye. Her hands shook where they lay flat on the table, and her voice shook when she spoke. "Wicca is a recognized religion in this country, and this state, with all the legal rights entitled to any other religion."

"The occult has been connected to a rash of vicious crimes in our town, Ms. Saint Angeline. Animals tortured and mutilated, vandalism and defacing of property, and most recently, it's been linked to the death of one of our own students. This is a serious cause for concern."

"There is no evidence whatsoever that any of the things you just named are connected to the practice of Witchcraft."

Sally Hayes' perfectly plucked eyebrows rose. "Well now, Bella, what are we supposed to think? That it's the local Baptists out there killing house cats in the graveyards in the dead of night?"

"That would be almost as ridiculous as assuming it was

the local Witches," Bella said. But though she tried to sound brave, all she could see in her mind was the dream. The townspeople standing around her, condemning her, watching her burn.

The principal seemed taken aback, but only for a moment. She recovered quickly, and said, "We're not here to determine who was or was not responsible for the crimes in town. We're here to determine whether or not, you, Ms. Saint Angeline, are a member of any occult group or organization."

Mirabella said nothing.

"Well?" the woman prompted. "Do you consider yourself to be . . . a Witch?" she said the last with a tone of derision, her words dripping sarcasm.

Mirabella looked her in the eye. "Keep fucking with me, Sally, and you're liable to find out."

An audible gasp went up from the people at the table. She knew damn well she should have held her temper. But Witch or not, she was only human. And this was illegal, immoral, and ludicrous. Bella got to her feet. "I'm a Wiccan, a Witch, a Pagan. It's legal. You cannot discipline me for practicing my religion. And I'm not even certain you can legally ask me about it."

"We can however, discipline you for speaking to your students about that so-called religion," Sally said. "Have you been doing that?"

"Of course not!" she blurted, almost before she thought about it. Then she frowned. "Not on school grounds and not in my capacity as a teacher."

"But you have mentioned Witchcraft to students, haven't you?"

She drew a deep, slow breath. "If a student asked me flat out if I were Wiccan, I may have answered yes. I certainly wouldn't have lied. If they asked what that meant, I might have given them a basic, honest answer. That's all."

Mrs. Hayes smiled slowly. "That's all we need."

"What do you mean?"

"Mirabella Saint Angeline, you are hereby suspended without pay from your duties as a teacher at Ezra High School, and forbidden to set foot on the premises, pending a full investigation of your behavior."

"You can't do this," Bella whispered.

"We just did. We will need to formalize this with a vote, of course. But at this point that's a technicality. It will be unanimous. Go to your classroom, gather your things, and go home."

# # #

Rowan glanced at the newspaper for the tenth time. Jonathon knew the headline by heart. "Local Teacher Suspended on Charges of Witchcraft!" He'd tried to trash the evening edition before his daughter caught sight of it, but she'd snagged it from his hand the minute he started for the fireplace with it. Almost as if she were reading his mind.

"Dad, we have to do something," she said.

He'd been thinking the same thing. The question was, what? He'd insulted Bella last night, called her most cherished beliefs so much bullshit. He doubted she would want his help. And even if she did, he wasn't sure what he could do.

"I'll try calling her again."

"Good."

He went to the phone, dialed the number, once again getting a busy signal for his trouble. He hung up. "Still busy."

"That's over an hour. Something's wrong."

He smoothed his daughter's hair. "Hon, don't jump to conclusions. She may have been getting some phone calls she didn't want. She probably took it off the hook."

Rowan grimaced. "Yeah, I can just imagine the kinds of phone calls she was probably getting."

He could too. And he didn't like what he was imagining.

"We should go over there, Dad."

"Honey. . . . " He pushed a hand through his hair. "I just don't think . . . ."

Rowan tipped her head to one side, searching his face with her laser beam eyes that were so much like her mother's it was uncanny. "Tell me the truth. Why don't you want to go over? No . . . you *do* want to go, don't you? You just don't want *me* to go."

He sighed. He couldn't lie to this kid. It just wasn't possible. "I'd rather not drag you into something until I'm sure of the situation. I don't know what's going on over there right now, and–"

"And you're overprotective and hyper to boot. Fine. I'll stay home. Just so long as someone goes over."

"I'm not real comfortable leaving you here alone either, with all that's been going on."

The doorbell rang. Sighing and rolling her eyes, Rowan went to get it. And when she came back, she had her best friend Shauna at her side. Shauna looked old, for a teenager. Dark circles under her eyes and a washed-out look to her face. Poor kid. This hadn't been easy on her.

"Shauna wants to hang out here tonight, okay, Dad?"

"Sure. How are you Shauna?" He kept his voice soft.

"I'm gonna be all right, Mr. Hawthorne. I just wish it would stop hurting."

He reached out a hand to stroke the girl's hair. "It eases up in time. After awhile, you'll be able to remember the good times and even smile a little. I promise."

She looked up at him. "I guess if you can say that, then I have to believe it."

"It doesn't feel like it right now though," he said. "I know."

"Dad, why don't you go now? I won't be home alone, and Shauna and I will be fine."

He looked from one of them to the other. "You sure?"

"Yeah. We'll eat some junk food and talk it out."

He bit his lower lip. During the course of the investigation of her boyfriend, Shauna had been checked out, and there hadn't been any indication that she'd been involved in or even aware of Bryan's questionable activities. Hell, they never really found proof that he'd done anything more than be in the wrong place at the wrong time.

And Jonathon really *did* want to check on Bella.

And it was *only* a few blocks away.

"Okay," he said at last. "Okay, but don't go anywhere. And call if you need me. All right?"

"Sure," Rowan said.

"Thanks, Mr. Hawthorne," Shauna said in her hoarse-from-crying voice.

Jonathon left the girls and drove over to Mirabella's house. When he got there, though, he wished he'd come sooner.

A crowd had gathered outside. Angry locals and reporters. He couldn't have walked through them to the front door if he'd wanted to. But he didn't see Bella's car in the driveway anyway. She usually walked everywhere she went, if it was local. Probably, though, walking wasn't the safest prospect for her right at the moment.

His throat went a little dry.

He drove on past and tried to think where she might go, when she had every reason to doubt her welcome at any place in this town. Including his own.

Only one answer came to mind. So he drove there. To that little shop that had been vandalized the night before. He'd heard about it at work.

And her car was there. But the place was dark as a dungeon.

Frowning, Jonathon parked across the street, got out, and went over to the shop's front door. The town was dead tonight. Everyone was either shouting obscenities outside Bella's house or at the school gym for the town meeting that had been called to address the problem of Witchcraft in Ezra Township. He'd heard a rumor they'd located an old law on the books which made teaching Witchcraft to a minor a criminal act, with no maximum sentence. It had to have been left over from the seventeenth century when the town was first founded. Now some wanted to resurrect it, enforce it, and prosecute those who'd broken it.

He crossed the sidewalk and stared up at the old Victorian house. The front wall still smelled of new paint, and the window had been replaced. No lettering on it yet, though.

A soft sound drifted up from below, and something bunted his leg. He glanced down to see a black cat rubbing against him.

"Hey, you wouldn't be the missing Circe, would you?" He bent down. There was a tag dangling from the cat's collar, and he bet it had a name on it. He would like to be able to return one missing pet to its owner intact.

But when he reached for the cat, she dodged him, and trotted around the house. Frowning, he went after her. She didn't go far. In fact, after a few yards, she turned to look back and waited for him to catch up.

When he did, she didn't run off again. Just stood still and let him scoop her up. He glanced at the tag . . . then turned his head slowly.

The haunting sound of voices, chanting in an overlapping, ever changing cadence, caught his attention. He looked at the windows, where the sound seemed to come from, and saw the flickering dance of candlelight casting shadows. Shapes of women, moving.

And there was a door . . . and oddly, it was open.

He held the cat close, and silently, drawn in spite of himself, he went through the door into a back room of the house.

Chapter Eight

Rowan and Shauna sat in Rowan's bedroom, nibbling ice cream out of the carton. They reclined side by side on the bed, and the stereo played Blink 182.

For an hour, Shauna had been pouring her heart out about Bryan. How much she'd loved him. How much she was going to miss him. And crying. She'd been crying a lot. Rowan just listened and didn't worry about saying the right thing, because as Bella had told her, there really was no right thing. And she thought Bella was right. Talking it out did seem to be easing Shauna's mind a little bit. It made Rowan feel she was helping her, in some small way.

And then, out of the blue, Shauna said, "I just wish he'd never got involved with that whole mess. I mean, it wasn't worth it. It just screwed up his head."

Rowan tried not to look as alarmed as she felt. "What whole mess, Shauna?"

Shauna sniffled, wiped her eyes. "Nothing. I mean . . . I don't want his name being dragged through the mud, Rowan. He's gone now, you know? It would be too hard on his mom."

"I wouldn't want his mom to suffer any more than she already has. Or you either. Come on, I'm your best friend. If you don't get it out, it's just gonna keep eating at you until you do, you know."

Shauna blinked her red rimmed eyes. "It has been helping, talking to you. How'd you get so smart anyway?"

"Mirabella–Miss Saint A, I mean. She told me you were going to need friends who'd just let you spill it all out."

Shauna lowered her head. "I guess Miss Saint A's going through some garbage of her own right now, huh?"

"They suspended her from her job at school. It's all over the papers that she's some kind of cat-murdering devil-worshiper."

"That's so lame," Shauna said. "They're so stupid. She's the best teacher we ever had."

"I know."

"She wouldn't hurt a freaking fly, you know?"

"I know."

Drawing a breath, Shauna lifted her chin. "Rowan, Miss Saint A didn't have anything to do with those animals they've been finding all cut up."

"I know."

"Yeah, but . . . I mean, I *really* know it."

Rowan frowned. "How?"

"Because . . . it was Bryan, and a couple of other guys. Swear you won't tell!"

Rowan heard what she said, but it took an extra beat to sink in. It was that far beyond belief. When she could finally spit out words, she blurted, "Why the hell would he *do* something like that?"

"Because he was paid to."

Rowan frowned hard, and tipped her head sideways. "You mean it didn't have anything to do with any . . . occult stuff at all?"

"No, of course not. Bryan's only religion was football and that stupid old junk car he wanted to re-build. He was getting paid a lot, Rowan. I mean, it was nothing for him to have three or four hundred bucks on him all at once. When he started throwing all that cash around, I thought . . . I don't know, I thought he was dealing drugs or something. So he told me the truth. Someone was paying him a ton of money to kidnap cats and rabbits and stuff, and cut them up and leave them where they would be found. The guy gave him instructions too. How he had to make symbols in blood and stuff. It was disgusting."

"Jeez, Shauna! What were you thinking? Why didn't you *say* something?"

She looked shocked at Rowan's anger. "Hey, don't act like I'm the one who was killing animals!"

Rowan just looked at her.

Shauna lowered her head. "Bryan hated it. I mean, he felt awful about it. And he said he never tortured anything, like the papers say. He always killed them first, before any of the . . . other stuff. And he promised me he'd stop. Then the cops saw him that last night in the cemetery. And he got scared. He told the guy he was working for that he wanted no more to do with it. He wanted out, you know?"

"Yeah?" By now Rowan was facing her on the bed, gripping her hands hard, eager to hear more. "And then what happened?"

"Nothing. The guy said fine, no problem. Bryan seemed so relieved. I thought he was gonna be okay, you know?" Shauna lowered her head as tears welled up again. "I guess he just couldn't deal with the guilt of killing those innocent animals, though."

"Right. Bryan killed himself over some cats and bunnies."

Shauna burst into noisy tears, and Rowan hugged her and rubbed her shoulders while she cried. "I'm sorry. I shouldn't have said that, but don't you see how ridiculous it is? Shauna, you have to tell me something." She pushed Shauna back a bit, so she could look her in the eye. "Who was the guy paying Bryan and the others to do this stuff?"

Shauna shrugged. "Bryan didn't tell me."

"Well, we have to find out."

"Row! You promised you wouldn't tell anyone!"

Rowan gaped. "Hello? Shauna, are you telling me you still don't get it? Think, will you? Bryan is questioned by the cops. Then he tells this jerk he wants out, and twenty-four hours later, Bryan is dead. Doesn't that make you wonder, even a little bit, Shauna? Doesn't it?"

Shauna frowned. Then slowly her brows rose, her eyes widened, and her face went even whiter. "Oh my God . . . do you think . . . ?"

"I don't know. But I think we'd better find out. Don't you?"

"I said all along Bryan would never kill himself! God, Rowan, what are we gonna do?"

"We have to find out who the guy was. Maybe the other kids involved would talk. Did Bryan say–?"

"No. No, he wouldn't tell me any details." She licked her lips, eyed Rowan. "Maybe there's something in Bryan's room. I mean, he kept journals–and I think this guy e-mailed him too. We could check his computer." Then she lowered her head. "But the cops have probably already done all that."

"No. No, it was ruled a suicide and blamed on Witchcraft. They didn't dig too much farther once all that was decided. Will his mom let us in his room?" Rowan asked. She seriously doubted it.

"She's not home. My mom took her out. She . . . she wanted a new suit for Bryan to wear for . . . for the funeral. She just couldn't bear to do it alone. That's why I came over. I couldn't make myself go with them, but I didn't want to be alone either."

She started to cry again.

Rowan gripped her shoulders. "I know. It's awful, I know. But come on now, pull it together, Shauna. Get a grip. For Bryan."

Sniffling, Shauna nodded, got hold of herself.

"Can we get in, Shauna? Can we get into Bryan's house, his room?"

"Yeah," she whispered. "He always left his window unlatched, in case I wanted to come by to say goodnight."

Rowan nodded, even though that sentence had her tearing up almost as much as Shauna was. "All right," she said. "Okay then. Listen, I can do this myself if you're not up for it."

Shauna dashed the back of her hand across her eyes, and got to her feet. "I'm in. If someone killed Bryan, I damn well want to know who."

They grabbed jackets, flashlights, and they headed out into the night. But when they got to Bryan's house, someone else was already there.

# # #

Jonathon walked silently into the large room, the cat nestled in his arms. A group of women stood in a circle, holding hands, and they didn't even notice him there. They were faces he knew. Granny Kate. Dr. Plummer. One of the secretaries from the DA's office, for crying out loud.

Mirabella was in the center of the circle. And he'd never seen her look like she did then. Her dress was simple, white, draping, tied with a braided cord of three colors. Her hair hung loosely down her back. She wore several necklaces, all of them laden with gemstones. Amber and jet. Moonstone and citrine. Others he couldn't have named. She stood with eyes closed, head tipped slightly back, arms up and out to the sides. The candlelight painted her face. And in spite of himself, he thought she looked more beautiful than any woman he'd ever set eyes on.

The other women chanted, their song falling into so many layers of harmony he couldn't separate one from another. It was beautiful. They sang the names of ancient Goddesses, and he thought he heard the sea, but there was no source for that. The smoke of incense filled the air. And there was something else. Something different about the space in the room where he stood, and the space within that circle of female bodies. That circle was different somehow, denser or . . . or something.

But then he couldn't focus on that, either, because the chanting stopped all at once, and Mirabella turned to her left and spoke, but her voice was different, deeper, richer, almost ethereal.

"Ashley Rowan Hawthorne, I stir thy spirit! Come ye forth, from beyond the Western gate! Bring thy message now! For the sake of thy daughter, come!"

And the others began to chant again, only this time it was his dead wife's name they sang. Over and over again, they said it.

Tears boiled from Jonathon's eyes, rolling down his face. He opened his mouth to shout at them, to forbid this nonsense. But before he could uttered a sound, he saw something. A swirl of particles, dustmotes or atoms, gathering like a misty whirlwind right in front of Mirabella. And when they solidified, she was standing there. Ashley. She was filmy, and thin, but there.

Jonathon whispered her name in a harsh voice and lunged forward. But he hit some invisible barrier when he would have forced himself between the women in the circle. Some shield that wasn't solid, but pressed him back all the same.

Mirabella's eyes were still closed. But she drew her hands in, turned her palms out, and as Jonathon stared in wide-eyed wonder, Ashley pressed hers misty hands flat to Bella's.

"What do you want me to do?" Bella asked.

"Love her." It was a long drawn out whisper, like the sound of a breeze in treetops.

"I *do* love her."

"Save her," Ashley whispered, long and slowly.

"How?"

Ashley's arms slid around Bella. It looked as intimate as an embrace between sisters. But he could see . . . or sense . . . her lips moving near Bella's ear. And then there was a wind, so strong it sent the door banging against the wall behind him. The candles went out in a whoosh. The cat leapt out of his arms.

He couldn't see Ashley or Bella any more, and frantically, he searched for the light switch, and found it.

With a flick of his hand, the room was flooded with light. Bella was sitting on the floor, shaking her head as if stunned. Gwenyth, the blond who owned the shop, stooped as the cat ran to her, and she scooped the animal up with a shout of joy.

Bella got to her feet, saw him and started forward, looking dazed.

"Cut a door!" someone yelled, and the woman in front of Bella traced an arch in the air.

Bella moved through it, and straight to Jonathon.

"What the hell just happened here?" he asked, and his voice was strained to the point where he could barely form audible words.

"We have to go. We have to go to Rowan."

He barely heard her. He was still staring at the spot where he'd seen Ashley. "Was that . . . how could she . . . *Ashley's dead...."*

"There's no such thing as dead."

"But . . . but . . . ."

She slapped him. Her palm was hot, he noticed, and it didn't sting much. Just enough to make him focus on her.

"Rowan is in trouble. We have to go. *Now*." She spoke with authority and power he'd sensed in her, but never seen before. And he found himself believing every word.

He nodded, still too stunned to speak. Mirabella took his hand firmly in hers and pulled him along toward the door. Over her shoulder she called, "Take up the circle. Call the police and send them to Bryan Marcomb's house. And hurry."

And the next thing Jonathon knew he was being tugged out the door, around the house to the driveway where her car was parked. She opened the passenger door and shoved him into the seat. Then she went to her side and got behind the wheel. A second later, they were speeding through town.

Chapter Nine

Rowan was standing outside Bryan's house, pushing up his bedroom window with Shauna tight to her side when she saw something moving inside the room.

She went stiff and still.

"What?" Shauna whispered.

Rowan backed up, pulling Shauna with her. "Someone's in there."

"Did they see you?"

"I don't know. I don't—" The window was yanked open, and a dark form filled it. "—Think so," Rowan finished.

The two girls turned to run, but Rowan could hear the footfalls behind them. And in less than a second a big hand hit her hard, right between the shoulder blades, and sent her face-first into the ground.

She rolled over onto her back, crab walking backwards from the man looming over her.

"Mr. Hayes," she panted. "What are you . . . why are you—?"

Shauna screamed for all she was worth, and Rowan looked toward her, only to see Mrs. Hayes, their own high school principal grabbing hold of her.

The man reached for Rowan, and she flung up a hand like a stop sign. She didn't know what made her do it, but every part of her was focused on one thing. Pushing him away from her. And though she never touched him, he went backward, staggering, then falling. She scrambled to her feet, turned to run, and hit a solid chest.

#

Jonathon saw his daughter send the attacker stumbling backward. And sure, he might have tripped, or just lost his balance. But he didn't think so.

He and Mirabella had sped straight here, heard Shauna's scream, and ran like the wind into the backyard just in time to see Hayes fall on his ass. Then Rowan was on her feet, turning to run. And then she was in her father's arms.

She jerked back, doubling up a fist and raising it. Then she blinked at him and hurled herself against him all over again. "Daddy!"

Beside him, Mirabella was holding a shaken Shauna, calming her. Sirens wailed, not that the police were overly called for. A coven of Witches had thundered into the yard only a minute behind him and Bella, their robes dancing in the night wind, their hair smelling of sandalwood. Several of them were hauling Mr. Hayes to his feet, while a handful of others were busily subduing Mrs. Hayes, who had released Shauna and tried to run for it.

Officer Billy Cantone came running. He took in the women, most of whom he knew, all of whom were dressed in ritual robes and jewelry, many of whom wore five pointed stars on chains. "Just what the hell is going on here?"

Mirabella stepped forward. "I think I can answer that. Mr. and Mrs. Hayes have been very eager to purchase my friend Gwenyth's house, on the edge of town. You know the one? Mr. Hayes has Gwen's permission to fish in the stream out back. And he made his first offer shortly after she first gave him that permission, this spring. He wanted the house very badly. Didn't you, Mr. Hayes?"

He grunted, and looked away.

"She turned him down. So he decided to get her run out of town. And since she was openly Wiccan, what better way to do that than to orchestrate a few ritualistic animal sacrifices, get the locals all stirred up over the Witches in their midst? Hmm?"

Sniffling, young Shauna lifted her head. "You were the one paying Bryan Marcomb to kill those animals that way, mess up the tombstones, and all that?"

"You bet he was," Rowan said. "And when Bryan wanted out—threatened to tell the police everything unless you let him go, you killed him. Didn't you?"

Jonathon stroked his daughter's hair. "And then you came back here to get rid of any evidence of a connection between you and Bryan," he said, as his mind filled in the blanks.

"My God. Is this all true?" Officer Cantone asked.

"I'm sure we'll find the evidence, either on these two, or still in Bryan's room," Jonathon said. "But what I don't understand is why? Why is one piece of property worth more than a young boy's life? Hmm?"

"It's the pyrite in the stream out behind the house," Mirabella said softly. She walked over to where her friend, Gwenyth stood looking puzzled. "It's not really pyrite at all, hon. It's the real thing. Gold. And Jim Hayes knew it. And he wanted it all for himself."

The cop's eyes widened. "How do you know all that, Miss Saint Angeline?"

She looked at Jonathon. And he knew. He knew these were the things that his wife had whispered to her in that magickal circle. How else could she have figured it all out—or known to come here, now, just at the moment when his daughter's life was in grave danger?

"An old friend told me," Mirabella said softly. "She uh . . . prefers her name be kept out of this. It's nothing you can't verify, after all."

"Arrest those two, Billy," Jonathon instructed. "And get some men out here to go through Bryan's room for evidence. We'll take the witnesses' statements tomorrow. It's been . . . a long night."

Billy cuffed Mark and Sally Hayes, and escorted them to the waiting cruiser. Mirabella turned to Jonathon, to Rowan. "It's done." And then she turned, and walked away.

#

There was no doubt in Bella's mind that, given the chance, the Hayes couple would have taken Rowan, and perhaps Shauna as well, killed them, and tried to make it look like suicide. Or maybe an accident. And if they had succeeded, it would have been one more crime for the good folk of Ezra Township to lay at the feet of the local Witches. And possibly, at Bella's own feet.

But thanks to one determined mother's love for her daughter, it didn't turn out that way.

Bella got all the way to her car. The others were pulling away now. The police car. The vehicles of her friends and sisters. She stood there, listening to the motors fade in the distance. Then to the crickets chirping and the gentle breeze whispering through the trees.

And then the breeze changed. It whispered "Mirabella . . ." in a voice that was becoming familiar.

Ashley's voice.

Closing her eyes to prevent tears, Bella said, "I saved her. What more do you want from me?"

"Save *him* . . . ." the trees seemed to whisper.

Bella opened her eyes, a trill of alarm running up her spine. "How?"

"Love him."

Damn. Why did her heart have to hurt so much? "I already do," she said softly, and she turned, and he was standing there.

"I'm sorry," Jonathon said. "I was wrong. I was wrong about everything. I was wrong about your faith, your beliefs. I was wrong about Ashley and about my own daughter. But most of all, Bella, I was wrong to ever let myself think for one minute that I had any choice at all about loving you. Because I didn't. And I don't."

She lifted her brows, tipped her head back to search his face.

"I need you," he told her.

Beside him, Rowan said, "We both do."

Bella blinked as her eyes filled with tears. "I . . . I don't know what to say."

"Say you'll marry me," Jonathon said.

Rowan clasped her hands together, pursing her lips and blinking her own tears back as she waited to hear Bella's answer. She might even have been holding her breath.

Mirabella smiled. "I'll marry you."

He swept her into his arms, and kissed her deeply. And then they parted just enough to enfold Rowan in their arms as well.

"Take care of each other," the breeze whispered.

Rowan pulled free of them, and looked up toward the sky. "We will, Mom. Thank you. Thank you for sending Mirabella to me."

Bella, arm in arm with Jonathon, went to her. "Don't think she won't be back, just because this little crisis is over," Bella said softly. "She'll always be with you, Rowan. And so will I."

Jonathon shook his head. Rowan and Bella both looked at him, and he had tears in his eyes. "I don't know what I ever did to deserve to have three such incredible women in my life." His voice was choked with emotion. "But I'm so glad I did it, whatever it was." He looked at Rowan. "Because I love you. I love you so much." And then he turned to Bella, cupping her face in his hands. "And you . . . you saved my heart. My soul. You made me live again. I didn't think I could love this way twice in a lifetime. But Bella, I do. And I believe you, what you said before. This isn't the first time around for us."

"No, it isn't," she told him. "And it isn't going to be the last."

# # #

About the Authors

Maggie Shayne

This mega-talented author sold her first novel to Silhouette Intimate Moments on August 24th, 1992 under the name Maggie Shayne. Since then she's published 26 books with 4 different publishers. She's currently writing for Silhouette and is a lead author for Berkley's Jove division. Maggie has been a RITA finalist several times and has won dozens of awards for her novels.

A Wiccan priestess, Maggie is probably most famous for her Vampire stories for Silhouette Shadows and Mira Books. She is steadily gaining recognition for her Immortal High Witch novels for Jove, including ETERNITY, INFINITY, and DESTINY.

.

Lorna Tedder

Lorna Tedder is the author of more than a dozen books. She holds a Ph.D. in Metaphysics and sells pagan fiction and non-fiction guides. She has been a world conqueror, an American revolutionary, and a 6th century Druid priestess. She hopes to make a difference in this life, too.

You can find her free articles and the occasional free book at www.spilledcandy.com

Maggie's witch books

Can't get enough of Maggie's witches? Try her witch series from another of her publishers, Jove Books.

ETERNITY -- ISBN 0-515-12407-9 -- $6.99

Her name was Raven St. James, a woman whose unearthly beauty and beguiling charms inspired rumors of Witchcraft. Only one man tried to save her from the hangman's noose--Duncan, the town minister, who thought it strange that anyone could accuse this lovely and vibrant woman of anything wicked. Stranger still was the fact that Raven was a Witch. And even though she held the power to save herself, she could not rescue Duncan--who died trying to help her....

INFINITY -- ISBN 0-515-12610-1 -- $6.99

For five centuries, Immortal High Witch Nicodimus has been suspended in an eternity of darkness. His heart was stolen away in the ultimate betrayal by his love, Arianna. Now Arianna discovers a way to bring him back. But the power that returns Nicodimus to her arms also summons an ancient enemy. To fight this dark danger, they must confront the past--and reclaim infinity....

DESTINY -- ISBN 0-515-13013-3 -- $6.99

She is Nidaba--an Immortal High Witch so ancient, so legendary, that for thousands of years she has been the ultimate prize, relentlessly pursued by Dark Witches. After more than four thousand years, her destiny has finally found her....

Ask your favorite bookstore for these books or call Jove (Penguin Putnam)'s toll-free number, 1-800-788-6262.

Looking for some *witchy* music?

Maggie and Lorna recommend...

the music of
David Wood
of Wytchwood Music.

Whether you want to dance to it, drum to it, or cast a spell to it, each of David's songs is unapologetically Witch music. Some could easily be theme songs for Maggie and Lorna's books. Others are audio spells cast before your ears.

Find out more about David Wood and how to purchase his witchy songs at

www.DavidWoodMusic.com

Witch Moon Waning
by Lorna Tedder

Chapter One

A stormy night in 1975
City Hospital

He was no ordinary witch.

He was eight pounds, eleven ounces of destiny nestled against her breast.

Lydia Stevenson sighed and leaned against the crisp, hospital pillows. He was the most beautiful baby she'd ever seen. His skin was still red and splotchy. His fuzzy blond head had a bit of a lump on top where the doctors had used forceps to help ease him into the world. The doctors had warned her about that: at barely eighteen, her hips weren't fully grown and the baby was so big. Still, he was the most beautiful thing she'd ever seen.

She lay her cheek against the pillow and gently kissed the soft spot on the baby's head. He was perfect, absolutely perfect. Ten fingers, ten toes, and properly equipped in the diaper area. Yes, perfect. She touched the tip of her little finger to his palm, and his tiny fingers curled around hers. Oh, he was so beautiful!

"Thank you, Goddess," she whispered.

For just a moment, she looked away from the baby, out the eastern window to the moon high above the trees. One corner of the bright circle had dimmed. Two nights ago when she'd gone into labor, it had been full, a brilliant golden witch moon, a rosy halo across the lower quarter. Her mother had given her something to slow down the labor, or the baby would have been born then. Lydia had watched the moon rise again last night, imperceptibly waning, while she counted the minutes between contractions. With each pang, she concentrated on the future, all the while focusing on a vase of irises a hospital volunteer had placed in the window. Then tonight, moments before the baby's birth, she'd stared intently at the flowers as the moon rose wide and glowing behind them, its red halo warning of impending danger. But everything had turned out okay. Her beautiful son had been born under a waning witch moon with a Rod Stewart song playing on a radio down the hall.

Lydia pulled the baby's blanket away from his feet and inspected his tiny toes and heels. The thermal cotton blanket smelled of baby powder and antiseptic. She ran one fingertip along the smooth sole of his foot. Those were feet that would tread dangerous grounds one day. She could see them in her mind, all grown-up and older than she was now, wearing a soldier's boots. Tears stung her eyes. His life would not be easy, but his destiny would not be like those of other little boys. He would be a powerful witch, more powerful than Lydia herself. And, though she could hardly believe it, more powerful than Mama.

The door to the hospital room opened, and a nurse stuck her head through. She looked enough like Lydia to be her older sister. "How are you two doing?"

Lydia nodded and smiled a little. "Fine." Her voice sounded so young to her own ears.

"Great. I'm Maddie. I'll be your nurse tonight. Visiting hours start in another ten minutes. Would you like me to take the baby back to the nursery?"

Lydia grimaced. "No! Why? Do I have to send him back?"

Maddie shook her head hard enough for a strand of blond to fall free. She'd pinned her curly hair out of her eyes, which were heavily painted with blue shadow. She looked very neat and professional. Lydia thanked the Goddess for a friendly face.

"You can keep your baby with you for as long as you like," Maddie told her. "It's just that most first-time mothers are a little intimidated by something so little and so fragile, and they try to get as much rest as possible while they're here."

Not me, Lydia thought. *Every minute with him is precious.*

"I'll wait until I'm sleepy." That would be a while yet. She was exhausted from childbirth but exhilarated at the same time. A good kind of tired. She still couldn't believe the miracle of this tiny life in her arms—or that such a large baby had grown inside her. Without the usual squirming and kicking, she felt a strange loneliness in her chest, almost as if she'd been abandoned or cut off from the life that had shared her body. She hugged the baby gently against her. Maybe when she felt sleepy, she'd have an easier time handing him back to the nursery. "I'll keep him just until I'm sleepy," she cooed to the baby in her arms.

"Good idea!" Maddie's head bobbed in agreement. "Are you ready to give him a name? I'll bring you the forms."

A name. How could she name him without Jacob?

"Not yet. I have to talk to someone first."

"The baby's father. Of course. What does he think of the little one? Is he a proud papa?"

Lydia's eyes brimmed. Jacob had disappeared three weeks ago.

Maddie must have seen the tears because she took a step inside the room. "Aw, honey, are you okay? Do you need something for the pain?'

Just Jacob.

"They gave you something a little while ago. It should be kicking in soon. Would you like me to get you a soda?"

Lydia nodded, knowing Maddie would scurry out of the room and that soon enough some medication they'd given her would make her sleep when all she wanted to do was stare at the baby, but Lydia didn't care. She wanted to be left alone with the baby, even for a few minutes.

The door swung shut, and Lydia cast a pleading glance at the moon. Yes, Jacob was all she needed. Jacob and the baby. If she had them both, she would never be left wanting.

She saw the baby then, under another waning moon of centuries past, as a man full-grown. He ran his coarse fingers over the white splash of hair on the face of a grand, black horse. The woman astride the animal beamed down at him, long dark hair at her shoulders and a wildness about her face. She raised her sword to the gods and shouted something in a language Lydia somehow knew was no longer spoken.

Lydia blinked and saw the baby again, under a waning moon of the future, as a man full-grown. He looked so much like Jacob! His blond hair had been trimmed soldier-short, and he wore unfamiliar weapons at his waist. He clutched at a young woman with wild blonde hair and swallowed the need to beg. Lydia couldn't see the woman's face, but she was thirty-ish and slim. Her name was…Lorelei…and the fate of the planet trembled in her hands.

"If you succeed," he told Lorelei, "you'll be an international criminal. And if you fail, we will all die. Either way, I'll never see you again."

"Then marry me now," she said.

Lydia blinked and the vision was gone. It wasn't the first she'd seen. It was almost as if they had arrived with her awakening hormones. Ever since the pregnancy's first month, she'd been attuned to memories of the past and of the future, memories that weren't hers. No, this child was no ordinary witch.

She rubbed her fingers over his toes and began to sing. "Earth, my body…." She let her fingertips travel up his tiny legs. "Water, my blood…." She reached his chest, barely rising and falling under her touch. "Air, my breath…." Then she kissed the soft spot again, the seventh chakra. "And fire, my spirit." She repeated the movements, the song.

> "Earth, my body; Water, my blood;
> Air, my breath; And fire, my spirit.
> Earth, my body; Water, my blood;
> Air, my breath; And fire, my spirit.
> Earth, my bod—"

"Singing, I see," interrupted a voice from the open door. "Aren't you taking to this motherhood thing a bit prematurely?"

"Mama," Lydia breathed. Dread wound its way up her fragile spine. She shifted in bed as if to shield her baby from harm.

"Hmmph. The nurse said it was visiting hours and I could come in. She said I could bring you this." Mama set a can of soda on the nightstand.

Lydia nodded once. She didn't trust Mama, and that hurt

more than she could ever say. They'd been best of friends for as long as she could remember, but Mama hated her now. Worse. Mama hated the baby. And especially Jacob.

Mama crossed the room in a swoosh and stood over the bed. Lydia could feel the power seeping from the woman's veins. Evelyn Stevenson was a High Priestess with a very old and prominent coven in the Wiccan community. She was fair and giving, but not to be toyed with. Or shut out. For the first time in her life, Lydia was genuinely scared of her own mother.

Mama waved her left hand over the baby. Her scowl melted away. "He's…everything I imagined."

Lydia held her breath. Wiccans in general—and her mother in particular—loved Nature, children, and all of life. They wouldn't hurt a fly. Yet Mama had surprised her, raging at Lydia for getting pregnant. Lydia could have understood it if Mama had been a fundamentalist Baptist ready to cast out a wayward daughter. But Mama wasn't usually like that. For heaven's sakes, the woman had founded a local charity for pregnant teens! Mama was understanding, kind, generous. Except where this baby was concerned.

"Mama…? You won't…*hurt* him, will you?"

Mama sat down on the edge of the mattress. She didn't take her gaze off the baby. Slowly, she shook her head. "No. I won't hurt him."

"Promise?"

Mama locked gazes with her. Something weary and fearsome burned behind her eyes. "Promise."

"I-I'm sorry if I disappointed you and Daddy."

Mama shook her head again. "Lydia, you could never disappoint us. We just didn't want you to suffer for your mistakes. Don't you worry, now. I've talked to Dad, and we'll raise the baby ourselves."

Lydia gaped. Her chest tightened. She couldn't breathe. "But—"

"You'll go to college in the fall just as we planned. You can lead a nice, normal life. Get your law degree, help people who can't help themselves, *marry* someone. You can have other children if you want. But I'll raise this one as my own." She reached for the baby.

"No!" Lydia turned sideways in the bed, her shoulder raised to protect the child. "This is *my* baby. Jacob and I will raise him together."

She must have cuddled the baby too hard against her because he started to cry. And didn't stop. The harder Lydia jiggled the baby, the harder he cried. Mama leaned forward and rubbed a soothing hand across his cheek. The baby turned toward her hand, rutted for it, and stopped crying.

"Here," Mama said, handing Lydia the four-ounce bottle of formula on the nightstand. "He's hungry."

Defeated, Lydia took the bottle and plopped the nipple into the baby's mouth. The baby sucked hard and then, finding the milk, opened his unfocused eyes. Lydia sniffed back indignation and hurt. She felt so damned inept. Anger boiled up inside her, made her shake.

"Mama, I want you to leave. This is my baby, not yours. I'm eighteen now, and Jacob and I are going to get married as soon as…as soon as…."

"Sweetie, Jacob's gone." Mama almost looked hurt when she said it, as if she felt bad about it. "You and Jacob are not meant to be together in this lifetime."

"Don't! Don't say that! We are!" Tears spilled down Lydia's cheeks.

Mama sighed and didn't say anything for a long time. "Sweetie, I love you more than anything else on Earth, and it's because I love you that I've tried to spare you any pain. I will *not* lose you. But I know that you and Jacob Colter aren't meant to be together. Some lives intersect only once. And this-" she patted the baby's bottom—"was the intersection of your lives."

"I don't believe that. I won't. I *can't.*" Lydia's voice went hoarse. Jacob was her life, her soulmate. She'd known it from the first time she'd laid eyes on him.

"I know it's hard, but I've seen it. Remember, I have visions; *you don't.*"

Lydia didn't say anything. What Mama didn't know wouldn't hurt Lydia.

"Sweetie, how do you think I knew about the wedding?

It broke my heart to see you standing there, waiting for a man who never came. He's not coming back to marry you. I've seen it, and you two will never marry. Never. You've got to face that and move on."

Lydia shook her head. She was sobbing now, blubbering as she held the bottle for the baby. "Something must have happened. He wouldn't just leave without saying good-bye. He'll be back." After all, they'd been secretly handfasted five months ago, promising to love and cherish each other. Not that a pagan ceremony meant much to Jacob—he'd tolerated it out of love for her. When Mama had refused to let them marry, they'd planned to elope on her eighteenth birthday—three weeks ago. Only one of them had kept the appointment. What a disaster! "He wouldn't just leave me," she repeated.

"He doesn't understand the Craft. He doesn't believe in it, in *anything*. If you stay with him, he'll want you to give up your spiritual beliefs."

"Then I will if I have to."

Mama winced. "You don't mean that. You could no sooner give up your beliefs than—"

"Then we'll work it out. He doesn't have to believe like I do. It won't matter."

"It will. You'll have so many things you'll want to share, and Jacob won't understand."

"Then I'll perform a ritual to *make* him understand." Lydia regretted it as soon as she said it. Mama had warned her often. Tampering with another person's free will was unethical. The repercussions were harsh.

"Oh, sweetie." Mama plucked a tissue from the nightstand and wiped away the trails of tears on Lydia's cheeks. "Don't you see? Jacob has a destiny that doesn't include you. It's a great destiny. But he can't do it with you hanging on. And you have a destiny that doesn't include him." A single tear rolled down Mama's cheek. "And this little boy in your arms, he has the greatest destiny of all of us. But his destiny hastens the end of the world as we know it."

Chapter Two

Panting, Jacob stood in the rain. He was soaked to the bone. Heavy storm clouds flashed lightning on the western horizon and obliterated the stars. To the east, just beyond the hospital parking lot, a yellow moon rose to meet the dark bloom of clouds. It glowed in an almost perfect circle, this moon, but one side looked a little smudged. A reddish fog crossed it.

He smiled to himself. Lydia would have said the moon was a sign of some sort though he didn't believe in that kind of stuff. She liked the moon more than most girls he'd known in high school or even in college. Lydia always seemed to know exactly what phase the moon was in. She knew to the exact minute when it would rise and set. She was weird that way, but still he loved her.

His sneakers drenched, Jacob squished through a rain-filled ditch. He was cold and wet and couldn't stop shaking. Just a few more feet and he'd reach the dry, warm shelter of the hospital building—and Lydia.

Was it true what Lydia's father had said on the phone when he'd intercepted Jacob's call to Lydia? That she'd been taken to the hospital? That Jacob had a son?

God, he missed Lydia. She had one of those great smiles that could light up a room. He didn't normally date girls five years his junior, but when he'd met her two summers ago at a Medieval faire on his college campus, he'd fallen head over heels in love with her. It was almost as if they'd been together for lifetimes—if he believed in that sort of stuff.

Jacob trudged through the rain, pausing under the trees near the hospital door to look for cops. Yes, Lydia was the best thing that had ever happened to him. Smart, pretty. She'd convinced him to pull up his grades. She'd helped him focus on what he wanted out of life. She was uncanny that way—gifted with the ability to guide the lost. The only problem was that she dabbled in witchcraft.

Jacob smirked and shook his head. Okay, so she didn't

dabble. She really believed in it. Not him. Visions, spells, ritu-als, wands, Tarot cards—that was more hocus pocus than he needed. But even when he made fun of her so-called religion, she remained steadfast. And because he loved her so much, he would humor her. He just wanted to see her again, be with her.

Taking a deep breath, Jacob turned up the collar of his jacket and headed for the sliding glass doors of the hospital en-trance. He kept his head down. He was risking everything by coming here—his college degree, his career, his future. None of it mattered if he couldn't see Lydia. Still, he had to be careful. The police were probably out looking for him by now. He'd probably broken that deputy's nose....

Best not to ask at the desk, he decided. Two crabby-look-ing older women and a security guard chatted at the gazebo la-beled "Information." If the police were on to him, they'd be waiting for a scruffy-faced guy on the lam to ask for Lydia Stevenson's room number.

He squinted at a color-coded sign beyond the desk and walked faster. He spotted what he was looking for and then dipped into the first elevator. Jacob held his breath until the doors closed. His heart raced in his chest. He punched the button for the fifth floor—the one for the newborn nursery and the maternity ward—and waited for the elevator to rise. What he was going to do when he reached Lydia's room, he didn't know. How could he take Lydia and the baby back with him when he didn't have a car or cash? When he was running from the police?

Jacob stepped out onto the floor of the maternity ward. Monitors beeped and buzzed in the distance. Nurses spoke in whispers at the linen closet. The heavy chemical scent of disin-fectants rose from floor, still damp around a "caution: wet floor" pylon, and stung his eyes and nose. Swallowing hard, he plod-ded down the hall, trying to look as inconspicuous as possible while his shirt and jeans dripped in his wake.

Babies. He stopped in front of a long row of windows that overlooked the nursery. Newborns. Six of them. All in clear, shallow tubs on rolling legs. Wrapped from neck down in a fuzzy, pastel flannel blanket. Miniature pink bows stuck to the soft down of hair on some of them. Flustered, he glanced from baby to baby. They all looked darned near the same, except for the four with pink bows. Girls, he supposed.

He squinted through the foggy glass at the two without bows. Lydia's dad had said the baby was a boy. Jacob could barely discern the lettering on Baby #4's rolling crib: Baby Boy Randolph. Not his. He peered harder, his heart pounding. That meant the last boy must be his. Why then did the tag say "Baby Boy Dennis?"

"Which one is yours?" a nurse asked, smiling at him. She was blonde and pretty and reminded him a little of Lydia except with longer hair. Maddie, according to her name tag. She crossed her arms over her pantsuit's white top and waited.

Jacob glanced from Maddie back to the babies, his gaze sweeping silently across the tags on each crib. His son had to be there somewhere! What if he wasn't? What if there wasn't a baby? Or if the baby wasn't here? What if this was all just a ruse to lure him into the open where he could be arrested again?

"What's the mother's name?" Maddie persisted. She had a kindness in her voice that he thought maybe he could trust. Maybe....

"Um, Lydia. Lydia Stevenson." If he'd had his way, it would have been Lydia *Colter* by now.

"Ah, of course. He even looks like you."

Jacob glanced back at the six babies. He frowned.

Maddie laughed. "He's in with his mommy right now. You know where they are, don't you?" She had a funny tone in her question. Did the nurse know?

Jacob shook his head. He had that antsy feeling in his stomach that he couldn't trust her after all. Or anyone. She was too helpful, too familiar. Almost as if she'd been waiting for him to arrive. She was hiding something.

"Oh, that's right." Maddie suddenly seemed to remember. "Her mother asked us to move her to a private room."

"Her...mother?"

Maddie eyed him suspiciously. She almost seemed to smile, and he wondered if she was flirting with him. Did he know her from somewhere? She noticed the wet blond hair at his shoulders, the damp jacket, jeans still dark with rain. "You haven't seen him yet, have you? Your baby?"

Jacob said nothing.

Maddie sighed and shook her head. "And your girlfriend? When was the last time you saw her?"

Girlfriend? "How did you know—"

"Shhh." Maddie put her forefinger to her lips. "I know who you are," she whispered. "And I know who your girlfriend's mother is. I disagree with what's happening here and I intend to set it right. Lydia's mother herself teaches her students not to tamper with another person's destiny without their permission, no matter how right the reasons. Unfortunately, she's too close to the matter to see that she's not abiding by her own convictions."

"Tamper with destiny? What are you talking about?" Jacob took a step backward. "Who *are* you?"

"I'm a good friend of Jonathon's."

"Who?"

"Never mind. Look at the far end of the hall, to the right of the exit sign."

Jacob slanted a quick glance at two men in dark suits, leaning against the wall and looking incredibly bored. The door between them led to a hospital room. "Lydia."

"This section of the hospital was built in the 1920's. It still has fire escapes on the outside of the building. If someone were to come up the fire escape and find the window open...."

She didn't have to say anything else. Jacob nodded and walked briskly back the way he'd come. Why Maddie-the-Nurse was doing this, he couldn't hazard a guess. Perhaps a disagreement with Lydia's mother. It had to be personal—and serious. Most people didn't put their careers on the line for a whim. For whatever reason, she must have had a burning need to correct things to put so much at stake.

In less than ten minutes, Jacob found himself inching across the slippery, rain-splattered railing of the fire escape. Rain peppered down on his shoulders. The last room on the fire escape—Lydia's room—lay closest to the end of the ramp. He watched from outside the window while a nurse in a white pantsuit thumbed open the locks on the window and left the room. Maddie.

Taking one last breath of wet air, he edged the window upward, just enough to crawl through, then lowered the window after him. The room was quiet, dim. A cough from one of the men in the hall reminded him how dangerous this was. He didn't care. He was alone with Lydia. No nurses, no cops, no Mrs. Stevenson. He tiptoed to Lydia's bedside and stifled a gasp.

She was beautiful, as always, and sound asleep. Blonde curls scattered across the pillow. She looked so pale and fragile against the stiff white sheets. She lay sideways, her knees curled toward her chest, and in her arms lay a tiny bundle of blankets. Something moved in their midst. A little mouth yawned wide. Blue eyes opened and blinked sleepily.

My son. Jacob clamped a hand over his mouth. *Oh, God. My son!*

It was the most incredible thing Jacob had ever seen. So small. He had Lydia's nose and pout, but the blue eyes and the arch of each eyebrow were as familiar to Jacob as his own reflection in the morning mirror. One tiny arm escaped the blankets and unintentionally bumped at the head of peach fuzz before resting against rosebud lips. The baby began to suck at his fist, not particularly knowing or caring that it was a fist or where it came from.

Humbled, Jacob smiled down at the baby. No doubt, this child was his. And so was Lydia. He had to find a way to come back and get them out of here. Maybe he could find a hospital chaplain to marry them. Then Lydia's mother couldn't keep them apart, even if jail could.

Lydia's eyelashes fluttered and opened. "Jacob?" Her eyelids seemed so heavy. She blinked several times to focus.

"I'm right here." He took her outstretched hand and kissed it.

"I thought I dreamed you." A lazy, drugged smile tugged at her mouth. "Are you really here?"

He kissed the bridge of her nose, between her dreamy eyes, and then centered a kiss on the top of the baby's head. "Yes, I'm really here."

"I knew you would come back for me. For us."

Her words tore at his heart. He swallowed the lump in

his throat. He couldn't take her away tonight. How could he? No matter how badly he wanted to.

"Lydia, I can't take you out of here. Not tonight. I-I don't have a car or-or *anything.*"

She didn't seem to hear. "Why didn't you come to the courthouse? I waited and waited until the justice of the peace said they had to close for the day."

He cringed. Did she really think he'd left her at the proverbial altar *on purpose?* "Lydia, I was— Lydia?" Whatever medicines they'd given her made her close her eyes and drift. "Lydia, can you hear me?" She nodded and opened her eyes, struggling to concentrate. "Lydia, I've been in jail for the past three weeks."

She struggled to shake off the effects of the medicines. "Jail? That's-that's impossible."

"Oh, it's very possible. And nobody in a small town wants to listen to a college kid with long hair."

Lydia tried to sit upright but gave up. "You're not a criminal. I *know* you."

He smoothed the fuzz on the baby's head and bent in close to kiss Lydia again. "It was a mistake, Lydia." Actually, it was a set-up, but this wasn't the time or place to discuss his suspicions. "I was on my way to meet you and got pulled over in the edge of Carson County. Okay, so I was speeding a little, but the sheriff insisted I was driving a stolen car. I showed him the records. They didn't match up with his. So they arrested me and held me until they could get it straightened out."

Lydia grasped his hand and squeezed. "I'm glad it's over."

"Um, Lydia? It's not over. I don't exactly have permission to be here with you tonight."

"You mean—?" She gasped. "You-you should go. Now. I don't want you in trouble because of me."

She was worth it. If he spent the rest of his life locked away, having this moment with her and their son was worth the risk. "I don't want to go," he said. "I want to be here with you. With both of you."

Lydia studied the baby's profile, then Jacob's. "He has your eyes, you know."

"I know."

"We'll get through this, Jacob. We *will* be together, no matter what Mama says."

That's what he thought. Mrs. Stevenson had something to do with his arrest. He'd been allowed only one phone call and Mrs. Stevenson had hung up on him. His parents were gone. He had no one. And his future mother-in-law had hung up on him. Even Mr. Stevenson had hinted that he knew where Jacob had been for the past three weeks, but at least the man was forthcoming enough—albeit tight-jawed—to tell Jacob of Lydia's whereabouts.

"You're right," Jacob conceded. "We will be together. All three of us. It just may take a little time."

"I'll wait for you." She squeezed his hand. "I will *always* wait for you."

He sniffed. He wasn't the kind of man who cried. "Have you named the baby?" he asked. Carefully, awkwardly, he lifted the bundle into his arms. Pride surged through him. His son. The best thing he'd ever done in his life.

Lydia nodded. "I haven't named him officially yet, but if it's okay with you, then yes, I've decided on a name."

"Anything you pick is fine by me as long it isn't some witchy name like Mephistophocles."

Lydia frowned, annoyed, but only a little. This wasn't a time to make fun of her love for all things witchy. Jacob instantly regretted his words. The medications forced her eyelids to close.

"He'll pick his own Craft name when he's ready," she mumbled.

Outside the door, someone spoke loudly to Lydia's bodyguards. He recognized the voice. Mrs. Stevenson.

"Lydia? Lydia, wake up. I've got to go." He laid the baby back in her arms, then kissed them both on the foreheads. "I love you, Lydia. Don't ever forget it. I love you."

"I love you, too," she whispered, eyes closed, as he lifted the window to step out into the night. "Jacob?"

One leg out the window, he looked back. Her eyes were open and shiny. "Yes?"

"I will never let you go. Never."

"I know."

"And Jacob?"

"Yes?"

"Jonathon. I'm going to name him Jonathon."

He smiled and nodded, then blew her a kiss. He saw the first tear roll down her cheek, and he turned quickly away. He couldn't bear to see her pain. He had enough of his own.

"Jonathon," he said aloud into the night air. He tiptoed toward the fire escape ladder. The railing creaked under his feet. He couldn't help smiling.

"I'm a good friend of Jonathon's."

Funny. He'd heard the name twice in one night.

He was too busy thinking about the coincidence to notice the deputies waiting at the foot of the fire escape.

Chapter Three

"Where is he?" Evelyn Stevenson screeched from the door of Lydia's hospital room.

The baby startled in Lydia's arms, and suddenly they were both wide awake. The baby scrunched up its tiny face and began to cry in airy, mewling yelps. His cheeks reddened to purple. Lydia jiggled him a little, but he wouldn't stop crying.

"Where's Jacob Colter?" Mama demanded again. She swooshed past the bed and craned her neck to look out the windows at the fire escape.

"Not here, obviously," Lydia said through gritted teeth. She jiggled the baby again.

"But he's been here. I can feel him." Mama reeled on one foot to glare at Lydia. "Not to mention, your dad told me Jacob had called for you."

"He has a right to see our son, Mama."

"My son, Lydia. *My* son. I told you, I will raise him myself. This is too important."

"Im-important? I thought you hated him." The baby

quieted. "Mommy's got you," she cooed into his ear. Then to her mother, she said, "And he is not your son. I won't let you raise him. Not as long as Jacob and I are around."

"You might not have a choice!" Mama snapped.

Oh, no. Mama held tremendous power in her hands. Lydia herself had seen some of her feats of magick. Mama kept complicated charts of moon phases, astrological time zones, and exactly when was the best hour to perform rituals for specific purposes. She always made sure to time her spells for maximum energy. If Mama wanted to work magick for a negative purpose.... She wouldn't do that though, would she? Mama knew the Law of Three, that whatever you send out comes back to you times three. What would it take to make Mama tap into the power of the Goddess to manipulate lives instead of save them?

Mama's frown softened. "Oh, sweetie, you're shaking."

Of course, she was trembling! Lydia had been brought up in a house that believed in Goddess and magick, but she'd studied Wicca for only a couple of years. The Craft deserved a lifetime of study. Lydia was still a novice, and no match for a High Priestess, especially when that High Priestess was her own mother.

Mama sat on the corner of the bed and, sighing, gazed at her daughter and grandson. "I love you so much, Lydia. As much as you love your own son. Maybe more because you haven't fully bonded with him yet. I love you as much as you love your Jacob. I would never wish anything bad on you, but things are coming that you can't see. Don't you understand, honey? I'm trying to protect you."

"All I see is someone intent on taking my son away from me."

"Sweetie, I'm trying to do what's best for you. For all of you."

Lydia looked away. She couldn't bear the sadness in her mother's eyes. In her heart, she knew Mama meant well, but sometimes she could be too over-protective. Why was Mama so desperate to raise the boy herself?

"You've got to trust me on this," Mama pleaded. She laid one hand on Lydia's shoulder. Her palm and fingers tingled with heat. She'd been working magick! She'd left the hospital not to get some needed rest, but to perform a ritual!

"Oh, Mama. What have you done?'

"Nothing I wouldn't do again." She looked haggard. Old and weary in a way Lydia had never seen before. Almost as if life itself were draining from her pores. "You'll understand when you're a mother."

"I *am* a mother."

"Not to this boy." She stretched out her palm to smooth his hair, but Lydia turned slightly, moving him out of her reach. Mama let her hand fall to the bed. "I won't let this happen. I *can't.*"

Lydia swallowed the panic in her throat. She'd never had to stand up to Mama before. In the past, they'd agreed on everything. They'd been the best of friends.

"Mama? You don't understand. I would *die* for this child."

"I know." Her eyes clouded. Her voice fell to a hoarse whisper. "But I'm not going to let that happen."

Mama leaned forward and touched the center of Lydia's forehead, at her third eye, her sixth chakra. Lydia startled at the energy that zapped into her brain. A vision overtook her, flattened her against the crisp, white pillows of her hospital bed. But the vision was distant, third-person, like someone watching over her.

A woman, running through the woods. Closer. A woman with blonde hair, fair-skinned. Leaping over a fallen log that was half-rotted and covered in a rug of green mold. Closer. A woman in her mid-twenties. The woman was barefoot, hopping from stone to stone across a bubbling, rushing, gurgling mountain stream. Her hair flew out in the wind and soaked up rising mist from the water. She flung herself into the air, coming down with a small boy in her arms, holding him above the water as it carried her down. Her clothes filled with water, dragging at her, tangling in brush under the water. Her arms tired. Her chest screamed. Closer. Her. Lydia. Drowning to save her son.

Lydia bolted upright in bed. She gasped, eyes widening. So that was what Mama saw when she looked at the baby! The death of her own child.

"There, there, sweetie." Mama stroked Lydia's hair. "It's all right. I'm not going to let that happen to you."

Gradually, Lydia caught her breath. Her face was wet with helpless tears. She reclined at last, the baby snuggled against her. "It doesn't matter, Mama. Thank you for showing me, but it doesn't matter. I would rather be this child's mother and have Jacob by my side for a few years and die young than to miss a moment with him. If I must die for my child, I'm willing."

"Then you do understand. I, too, am willing to die for my child."

Thunder rumbled in the distance.

Lydia started to say something, but the door opened. She and Mama both sniffed back tears. Lydia looked away, intentionally focusing on a bright, jagged lightning bolt that grounded somewhere in the woods to the east of the hospital. Dark clouds hid the moon.

A tall, willowy brunette in a white pantsuit trotted toward her with a clipboard. She sidestepped Mama and laid a plastic thimble of pills on the countertop. She poured water directly from the tap into a Styrofoam cup and turned back to Lydia. The nurse paused to flip her feathered hair off her cheek, and her well-sprayed curls all moved as one.

"Miss Stevenson? I'm Sandy. I'll be your nurse for this shift." She waited for Mama to pick up the baby, then handed Lydia the pills and the lukewarm water.

"Wh-what happened to Maddie?" Lydia asked. She took the little cup of pills and stared into it.

"Go ahead," the nurse urged. "Take them. I'm required by hospital policy to watch you swallow them."

"Why? What are they?"

"Codeine. They'll help relieve the pain and help you sleep."

"But Maddie said——."

Sandy frowned. "Who's Maddie?"

"The nurse. The blonde. She was here earlier. She said she was going to be my nurse for the evening." *She was nice,* Lydia almost added but didn't.

"We don't have a nurse named Maddie. You were probably dreaming."

Dreaming? No, Maddie was real. At least, she thought Maddie was real. Was Lydia really that out of it?

Sandy motioned impatiently for Lydia to swallow the pills. When Lydia didn't, the nurse lifted the hem of Lydia's hospital gown and pried her bottom off the mattress for a better look. Lydia scowled at her.

"I'll be back in a few minutes with an ice pack," Sandy said. "That'll help keep the swelling down. I'll take your baby back to the nursery then. But first let me see you swallow those pills."

Still glaring at the nurse, Lydia downed the two pills. She preferred Maddie. Maddie had been nice. Pleasant. Had so much time passed that Maddie's shift was over?

"Listen, sweetie," Mama said when Sandy had left the room, "I'm going to go home and call the coven. We have a Wiccaning to prepare for."

Lydia nodded numbly. She'd been to a couple of naming ceremonies Mama had presided over. A Wiccaning could be a very special time for a new Mommy and Daddy. But not for her. Not if Mama wouldn't let Jacob near her.

"I've already thrown some runes for the boy." Mama returned the baby to his mother's arms. "They show some interesting patterns in his previous lives. I think we should honor his past. What would you think about 'Gareth' for a good Breton name? Or 'Dwn' for his time in Wales?"

Lightning crackled outside. Lydia felt its call like a craving to be touched. "*I* want to name him."

"Okay. Okay, sweetie. I owe you that." Mama patted Lydia's knee and rose from the corner of the bed. "I'll be back in the morning. Meanwhile, I want you to start thinking about college. It's not too late to register for this semester, you know."

Lydia didn't look up as the door creaked shut behind Mama. She didn't have to. She could sense Mama's presence as it left the room, the floor, the building. Lydia bent to kiss the baby's soft spot.

She didn't know if it was the codeine—she hadn't eaten

anything solid in over two days—or maternal instinct or something far more fierce. Her blood seemed to tingle. Most over-the-counter medications that knocked the average patient out like a light worked the opposite for her. They buzzed through her bloodstream and gave her more energy than a kitchen full of coffee. When she'd had her wisdom teeth out, the pills had turned her into a one-woman cleaning machine for a solid five days. The prickling sensation on her skin made her wonder if history was about to repeat itself.

Thunder rumbled again. Sandy the Bitch had not returned with the ice pack, and Lydia didn't even want to think of where Sandy planned to stick that ice pack or how un-gentle Maddie's replacement would be.

Lightning sizzled through the night sky outside her window. It seemed to call her name.

Name. Mama wasn't going to name this baby. Lydia was. Right now. In her own naming ceremony.

She laid the baby gently on bed and then snagged her housecoat from the chair. The white terrycloth dragged the floor, but she didn't bother to belt it. She pulled the baby's diaper off and re-wrapped him in his thermal blanket. She drew him close to her. Tired as she was, energy surged through her body.

The maternity floor seemed deserted. The few nurses in sight were busily scratching down important information on clipboards. No one seemed to notice her as she slipped down the sterile hallway to the elevator. She was just another healthy young mom enjoying a walk with her baby.

Nor did anyone notice her in the lobby. The information booth had closed along with visiting hours. All the doors were locked from the inside, meaning no one could enter the building but last-minute visitors could exit. Lydia stared through the glass doors at the rain peppering down on the sidewalk. Lightning flashed in her blood. Thunder rumbled again, calling to her. She obeyed.

With the baby nestled against her breast, protected from the rain, she stepped barefoot into the night. She didn't run. The spot between her legs still ached terribly, and she couldn't have run if she wanted. The storm raged around her, dampening her robe at the shoulders. The hem dragged behind her in the mud. Her blonde hair fell in tangles at her shoulders.

She stopped atop a grassy hill due east of the parking lot. Her bare feet sank into the watery grass. Lightning sprawled across the sky. Thunder was close enough to shake the ground under her feet. She could feel the power of Nature all around. Mother Earth. The Ancient Ones.

Lydia opened the bundle in her arms, pulling back the blanket from the naked, squirming baby. He opened his mouth and scrunched up his eyes to cry, but no sound came out. She raised him high above her head, naked to the sky and cold rain and thunder and lightning and clouds and Universe. She blinked upwards at the sky, raindrops filling her eyes. Then she did as men and women of olden times had done.

"Ancient Ones,
Gods and Goddesses who watch and abide,
Hear me on this night.
In Your great show of power, of celebration,
I present to you my son
For whom I will die.
Make him Your instrument
To protect the Protector
And salvage this planet.
Give to him his destiny
As You give to me my own.
I dedicate now to Thee, O Ancient Ones,
My son, Jonathan Colter!"

The baby let out a wallop. Lydia closed her eyes as the rain pelted down on her face. It was cool and full of cleansing. Shimmering lightning flashed around them in a perfect circle. Thunder broke the night. The rain slowed to a drizzle, then faded to mist.

"What the hell are you doing!"

And then Sandy the Nurse was yanking the baby from her and screaming and cursing her and running for the hospital.

Chapter Four

A sunny afternoon in 1976
City Hospital, Psychiatric Center

Jacob held his breath and shoved through the heavy door. He expected to see bars on the windows. Instead, the interior of the Psychiatric Center looked more like a hotel lobby. It was clean and friendly, with plenty of light. A Rod Stewart ballad played softly over the intercom system. Lydia would've liked that—if she'd had a choice of being there.

Snakes of dread twisted in his stomach. He hadn't seen Lydia since that night at the hospital, that awful night when he'd been dragged back to jail. She'd been beautiful, radiant in her new motherhood, and exhausted all at once. How she could have done what they said, he just didn't know.

It was only by the grace of God—or actually, by the grace of Evelyn Stevenson—that he was allowed to visit Lydia today. He'd finished his time at the Carson County Jail for assault and battery on the deputy who'd tried to keep him from escaping to see his new son. The other charges—the false ones—had been dropped. He'd hitched a ride straight to Lydia's doorstep. He'd known it wouldn't be easy, but he'd never expected a negotiation.

"I'll make a deal with you," Mrs. Stevenson had offered. "You leave town without my daughter. I'll make arrangements for you to see your son whenever you want."

He'd turned her down, flat. He'd come back to find Lydia and *marry* her. He and Lydia were going to have a happy life together. They'd spend their evenings curled up by the fireplace, reading to their son and later to his brothers and sisters. When Jon woke from nightmares, they'd invite him into their bed to comfort him. Jacob would play horse-y on the living room floor, the little boy laughing and giggling as they plotted to scamper across the carpet and tickle Lydia's bare feet. Oh, but Jacob had dreams—and they all included Lydia.

"Very well," Evelyn Stevenson had concluded with a nod. "I'll also have your record expunged."

"Oh, yeah? What makes you think you can do that?"

"I have...*powerful* connections. I know from Lydia how important it is to you to have a career in finance and that you've lost that with your arrest. You must never forget that sense of helplessness. It will benefit you in the future when you're a revolutionary."

"You had something to do with that, didn't you?" he'd spat back. "With my being arrested."

"My consulting business will be happy to provide you with a position that coincides with your...unfortunate incarceration. Jacob Colter, you can have your future back."

"Just not with Lydia and the baby."

"That's correct."

"Ma'am," he'd said with bile rising in his throat, "without Lydia and the baby, I don't have a future."

He still felt that way now, even after Mrs. Stevenson had finally relented and agreed to let him see Lydia. But Lydia didn't come skipping out of her bedroom, baby in arms and proud to see him. Lydia didn't come out at all. Mrs. Stevenson let him walk through the entire house, calling Lydia's name, growing more desperate by the minute.

"Lydia's not home," she said finally.

He'd plopped down on the couch in the living room. "Then I'll wait for her and the baby to come home."

"You may have a long wait. Grandpa took Jon-Jon to the zoo. They won't be back until dark." Mrs. Stevenson's eyes had gleamed, then moistened. "And Lydia won't be home at all this month."

How could she have done that to him? Waited for more than an hour of tense conversation to tell him Lydia had been admitted—judge's orders—to the Psychiatric Center for observation. She'd done something wild and strange enough to upset City Hospital, the HRS Child Protection Unit, and a local judge who'd fretted that Lydia was a danger to her own baby. Her obstetrician had explained to the eager beavers at HRS that Lydia had simply had an allergic reaction to the damned codeine. At first, euphoric stimulation. Hallucinations. And then nausea so severe, she curled up in a ball and begged for sleep. Except that…there were…*other things* wrong.

Even now as Jacob strode down the bright corridor toward Lydia's room, he found himself frowning at what Lydia's doctor had told him when he'd asked permission to see her. Lydia Stevenson was depressed, prone to hallucinations, and possibly a threat to herself.

A threat to *herself.* His Lydia. The sweetest, cheeriest person he'd ever known. His guiding force. And the mind doctors thought she might do something to hurt herself?

A nurse met him at the door to Room 139 and punched in a four-digit sequence on the lock box. Jacob mumbled his thanks and pushed the door open enough to peer through the crack.

"Oh, Lydia," he whispered. Better if someone had sliced him through the heart with a dull knife.

She sat cross-legged on a futon and stared out the windows—which did have bars. She didn't seem to notice him there. She was barefoot as always, but this time she wore a thin, white shirt and elastic-waist pajama bottoms. Her nipples shone through the shirt.

Of course. No bra straps to…so she wouldn't…so she wouldn't…wouldn't….

His stomach churned. What could have happened to Lydia to bring her to this?

The door clicked shut behind him, leaving them all alone in an overly bright but sparsely decorated room. Lydia glanced up. Dullness painted her eyes. Then they sparked to life.

"Jacob!" She practically flew off the futon and into his arms. Throwing her arms around his neck, she buried her face in his shoulder and long hair. "I didn't think I'd ever see you again!"

"Me, either," he mumbled through stinging tears. He held her then, without saying a word, for what must have been forever. He didn't need to talk. Just holding her was enough. He'd forgotten the way her skin smelled, the silkiness of her hair. He kissed her wet cheek again and again.

Sometime later, when the room was less bright and shadows had started to move across the walls, Jacob pried her arms from around his neck and sat down with her on the futon. "We need to talk."

She gazed up at him through wet eyelashes that clumped together. "You have a halo," she said, smiling. She touched his hair, smoothed it from his face. "Actually, it's an aura. It's all around you."

What the hell? "Lydia, are you all right?" Probably a dumb question given her whereabouts, but the sudden glaze in her eyes chilled his blood.

She shrugged. "I can't make them stop."

"Make who stop?"

"The visions." She smiled suddenly. "Did you know Jon's going to look just like you?" Then the smile faded. "Promise me you'll take good care of him when I'm gone. He's going to need you more than ever."

"Lydia, stop it! We're all going to be together. The three of us. I'm going to find a way to make it happen." *If I have to strike a deal with the Devil himself or worse—with your mother.*

"No. You and Jon will be together. But I won't. I can't. I've seen it." Sunshine through the window moved across her face, leaving it in shadow.

"Shhh, don't talk like that. Ah, baby, what have they done to you?"

She frowned and lay her head against his shoulder. "They think I might hurt Jon. How could they ever think that?"

"Something you did the night he was born. What happened after I left? Your mother wouldn't tell me. Nor would the doctor. Just that you haven't been allowed to see Jon since then."

"I presented Jon to the Gods."

"The what?"

She lifted her head. Then, with rapt face, she described in agonizing detail how she'd felt a strange impulse to carry out an ancient ritual. She'd taken their newborn baby into a lightning storm and held him up to the dangerous bowl of heaven!

Jacob fought to tamp down the anger in his blood. "Lydia, why would you do such a fool thing?"

"It's his birthright. His dedication to the Gods. It was done for him in many lifetimes past. I couldn't deny it for him in this one. Our little Jonathon has a great destiny, and I wanted the Gods' approval of him."

Jacob blinked stupidly. Had Lydia completely lost her mind? *Oh, no.* "This isn't that Wicca shit again, is it?"

"It's much older than that. It's…ancient."

"Lydia!" He shook her. "You lost custody of our baby because of some lunatic belief in magic?"

She cringed. "Ah, if only you could see what I have seen. I've seen us together when we're old. I've seen you sitting beside my bedside, all worried and graying. I've seen—"

"Stop it."

"I've seen—"

"Lydia! Do you realize what you've done?" He could hardly believe it himself. "You've destroyed our future together. Your mother has temporary custody of our little boy and if I blow every dime I can beg, borrow, or steal, I might be able to afford a lawyer who'll help me get supervised visitation rights because I've spent all my son's life in jail. And the doctors and HRS are so scared of your talk of hallucinations that you'll probably never get anything but supervised visits with Jon." He gritted his teeth. "All because of this goddamned witchcraft shit!"

She pulled away from him. Tears welled in her eyes and spilled over. "Do you think I want this? Any of this? Trust me—I'd rather not know the past or the future. Jon in Medieval times. Jon in Scotland in some uprising. Jon at the turn of the next millennium. I didn't ask for these visions—they just came."

"Hallucinations, Lydia. Call them by what they are. There's no such thing as 'visions.'" The words came out hoarse and harsh. Damn it, but he was hurting, too! "The whole time we were dating, even after I asked you to marry me, you never told me you were having hallucinations. Don't you think you owed that to me? I could have gotten you help."

"I don't need mental help, Jacob. These things are real."

"Lydia—"

"I didn't mean to hide it from you. I tried to talk to you several times about my psychic visions, but you poo-pooed them so bad and made fun of me so much that I knew we couldn't talk about it. Jacob, I wanted more than anything to share this with you, but...." She shook her head and stared longingly out the nearest window. "Mama was right," she mumbled under her breath. "You don't believe in anything."

"I believe in us." He took her hands and turned her around to look at him. "When did all these hallu—um, *visions* start? Was it gradual? How long have they been bothering you?" *And how far gone are you?*

Lydia backhanded her tears. "They started right after I found out I was pregnant. I had morning sickness, remember? Couldn't keep anything down. I'd just come back from my OB/GYN's office. He'd given me a tranquilizer to help with the nausea, and I came home to lie down for a nap. I had this dream about Jon and a pretty blonde woman with a sword. Except that I was still awake."

"Tranquilizer? Why would a doctor give a pregnant woman a tranquilizer?" He snatched a tissue from the box beside the bed and then dried her cheeks for her.

"It's an anti-nausea drug. Also happens to be a tranquilizer. I stayed on those for five months until the morning sickness passed."

He stared at her. "And you were having these visions the whole time?"

"Yeah."

"What about when you stopped taking the tranq?" Something niggled at the back of his mind.

"What about it?"

"Did the visions stop?"

"No."

He vaguely remembered a purse full of medicine bottles. "But you were taking other pills."

She nodded. "Painkillers for my lower back when I was very pregnant. They made me woozy, but they were safer for the baby, the doc said."

"And then they gave you drugs when Jon was born. And codeine afterwards."

She nodded again.

"And every time you've been on any kind of drug that

makes you woozy, you see things."

She shrugged. "They make me let down my guard. Things—*visions*—come through my defenses."

"Lydia." He almost smiled as he spoke her name. "Before you met me or got pregnant, did you ever have any type of drug that made you woozy or out-of-it?"

She thought for a second, then slowly nodded once. "When I had my wisdom teeth extracted. They gave me Librium and later Darvon. Made me high and loopy-headed at the same time."

"And did you see things?"

"No, just...*dreams*." Her eyes widened. She wet her lips. "Dreams about a blonde woman with a falcon on her arm. Her name is Lorelei. Jacob! It's the same woman in visions of Jon in the future!"

"Oh, baby, I am so glad!" Jacob gathered her in his arms again, kissing her. "Do you realize what this means?"

She shook her head.

"Your hallucinations aren't coming from some terrible mental condition that requires you to be locked away. They're coming from heavy-duty drugs doctors prescribed for you. This is not your fault!" He kissed her again. For the first time in months, he felt a twinge of hope.

"You believe me then? That I'm seeing visions?"

"I believe you're seeing things that aren't there because you have some kind of odd intolerance for certain kinds of medicine, and the hallucinations are a side effect of those drugs." He sighed and pulled her close, then pushed her out to armslength. "Do they still have you on any kind of drugs, here, in this place?" He motioned around the room.

"They must." She smiled weakly. "I've been having conversations every day with a pretty blonde nurse everybody says doesn't exist. And Jacob? She's the one in my dreams. The woman with Jon. The one with the sword. Lorelei the Falconer. The High Priestess of the Remnants of Humanity."

He couldn't stand it. His Lydia, gone stark raving mad courtesy of the medical profession's idea of pain relief and sedation. He had to do something before he lost her completely.

"I'm going to get you out of here, Lydia. No matter what the cost."

Even if he had to give her up.

Even if he had to take the deal with Lydia's mother.

Chapter Five

An autumn night in 1980
City Hospital Cancer Ward

She hadn't seen a witch moon like that since the night Jon was born. Large, looming, waning.

Lydia pressed her cheek against the cold glass pane and through the window stared up at the night sky. Fresh air seeped in from around the window frame, and she relished every breath. She hated hospitals—*hated them*—with all their chemical fumes rising from the newly-washed floors. Twentieth-century healing techniques were…unnatural. Back in the sixth century, Jon and Lorelei had gone to the sea to soak in its antiseptic waters and heal a nasty battle wound. Healing waters no longer existed. They were all polluted, enough so that a quick bath in their slime would bring infection rather than healing it. The "cure" would be worse than the disease.

Just as it was with Mama's cancer.

The radiation, the chemotherapy, the drugs. Surely it would have been better for Mama if she and her coven had gone deep into the forest and serenaded her with ancient hymns while she drank a quick poison. This disease had been lingering…and devastating. The beautiful, vibrant, powerful woman had wasted to yellow skin and bones. Hair falling out in clumps. Hands withering to claws. Too feeble to lift a swab of water to her swollen tongue. This had gone on too long, too painfully. Death was welcome here but would not come.

Lydia had begged the coven to help, but the other priestesses had told her they were helpless to lend a hand—or a little spiritual energy. Evelyn Stevenson had blocked their efforts.

Evelyn Stevenson insisted on bearing the full brunt of her burden.

"You must be strong," someone said from behind Lydia.

She recognized the voice and whirled. "Maddie!" The petite blonde nurse, whom everyone insisted didn't exist, perched on the plushest chair in the deserted waiting room and gazed up at Lydia with big blue eyes. She called herself Maddie, but Lydia knew her name was Lorelei. *The* Lorelei.

"Time is short. You need to go to your mother now."

"She's sleeping. They don't think she'll wake up." Lydia choked back the tears. For all their differences over Jacob and the baby, Lydia still loved her mother more than her heart could bear.

"She'll wake up one more time. For *you*."

Lydia let out a ragged sigh. She'd lost too much in the past few years. Jacob. Daddy. And now Mama.

Thank the Goddess, she still had Jon, even though she was allowed to be with him only in Mama's presence, only in the evenings after college classes were over. Every weekend, Mama took the boy and disappeared to who-knew-where. It was a compromise Lydia could live with gladly so long as she had Jon in her life. Even if she couldn't be a mother to him. Even if she couldn't be with Jacob.

Mama had taken care of everything. The stay in the Psychiatric Center had been altered officially to blame an allergic reaction to drugs used in childbirth. In no time at all, Lydia had been registered in an accelerated program at the local university and was now only one semester from finishing law school. No one knew about her strange visions or out-of-wedlock child. Except Mama and Jacob. And Maddie.

"Where have you been?" Lydia asked, sitting down beside her old friend—imaginary or not. "It's been well over four years since I last saw you."

A frown plowed its way across Maddie's forehead. "Really? It's been that long?" She paused, listening to the nearly inaudible music over the hospital's speakers. Something mournful by Rod Stewart. Maddie nodded to herself, then shrugged. "I guess it has been."

"You were right. All I had to do was stop talking about my visions as soon as they took me off the meds, and the doctors all blamed the drugs for my 'hallucinations.'"

Maddie nodded knowingly. She had been a godsend during those lonely days at the Psychiatric Center. Always showing up in a white polyester pantsuit with a clipboard in hand, just as she had now. Lydia had also learned not to talk about Maddie to the Center's staff. They denied that a "Maddie" worked on their staff. Besides, she often showed up when Lydia had been locked in her room for the night and usually spoke in whispers just out of sight of the staff.

"I've missed you," Lydia said. "You were always there when I really needed you. I used to wonder if you were one of my spirit guides."

Maddie laughed. "No. You haven't met *them* yet. But I think you will."

Lydia studied the woman. Curly blonde hair falling freely into her eyes. Concerned blue eyes that pierced the wall around Lydia's heart and took on an ethereal glow. Heavy blue eye shadow over her lids, like they'd worn in the '70's. In fact, she looked exactly the same as she had every time Lydia had seen her.

"I know who you are."

Maddie startled. "Of course, you do. I'm your oldest friend."

"You're—you're Lorelei!" Lydia reached for her, but Maddie warily held up her clipboard as a shield.

"Go to your mother's bedside. *Now.* You have something to resolve." Maddie rose and strode out of the room.

"Wait!" Lydia ran after her. "When will I see you again? Wait! I need you—"

Maddie was gone. Lydia stood in the doorway of the waiting room. The corridor was empty. Maddie had vanished into thin air. Again.

Mama. Lydia dashed down the corridor to her mother's room. Visiting hours were over, but the nursing staff, knowing the end was near, had let her stay close by. Even before Lydia pushed through the door, she heard her mother's hoarse voice chanting.

"I bind you, Jonathon Colter,

From accepting your mother's magick.

I do this out of love for her and thee.

As I will it, so mote it be.

"I bind you, Jonathon Colter,

From accepting your mother's magick...."

Lydia raked in a sob. Mama lay frail and white against the bed sheets. Tubes that had filled her nose and mouth and the ravaged veins in her hands and arms had been pulled out, some leaving a bloody trail across the white linens. Mama's hair seemed dull and dust-like, what was left of it. Her sallow skin seemed to sink into the now bony face. Her eyes were closed, but she continued to chant, now little more than a murmur on dry lips. A living corpse.

But in her skeleton-like hands, she clasped a photo of Jon, black ribbon wrapped around and around it, binding him to her will. A bluish-purple aura shimmered around the entire bed.

"Mama?"

The aura faded. Mama opened her pain-filled eyes. She must have used all of her strength to rip out the tubes and cross the room to where her overnight case lay askew, its contents falling across a year-old magazine a volunteer had left. She'd known when she packed for the hospital that she would need a few last ritual tools, hadn't she?

"I...want this...buried with this body." She nodded, almost imperceptibly, at the photo and ribbon.

"Mama," Lydia wailed, falling into a straight chair beside the bed. "Why did you bind Jon from me?"

"Because I don't...have much time left...here." She tried to smile. Her dry lips cracked and bled.

Lydia snagged a tissue from the nightstand and dabbed the lips that had once kissed her goodnight. She fought her own nausea at seeing her mother this way. "Shhh, Mama, don't talk." It must have hurt to talk. Lydia could hear it in every syllable.

"I have to...do this...Lydia. Jon and his...soulmate...will usher in the Age of...Remnants."

Remnants? Lydia had seen the future, too. Lorelei—Maddie—would one day be the High Priestess of the Remnants of Humanity. And Jon would be at her side, the last best hope for a planet in the aftermath of destruction. It would be hard. It would be terrible at times. But Jon was the key to Mother Earth's survival.

"It's his destiny, Mama. You can't change it."

"I have…changed yours." Something vaguely resembling a laugh gurgled in her throat. "I'm paying the…price for tampering with destiny…so you don't have to. I love you that much…Lydia. I would…die for you. I…*am*…dying for you."

The light in her eyes flickered. Lydia seized the bony hands that had once tucked her in and promised to drive away nightmares. Now Mama herself looked like a monster from long-forgotten nightmares. Her fingers were hot with magick, but the wrists and arms were ice cold as life withdrew to her most vital organs.

"Don't say that, Mama. It's stomach cancer. It's not your fault."

"It is. I brought this…on myself."

"No. No, Mama. You didn't do this to yourself. Cancer victims don't willingly invite this kind of suffering on themselves."

"Most…cancer patients…don't. But I…did. I—" She paused to lick at her dry lips. "I v-violated…my own ethics. I broke the rules I…lived by."

"No, Mama—"

"I…changed your life's course without…your permission. I sent out so much negative energy…and it came back…threefold. I myself brought all these negatives into…my life…and this…this is how I manifested those negatives. As cancer. Eating away at my gut."

Lydia's forehead sank against the mattress. She'd known for years that Mama was working magick against her. Out of love, out of hate—she hadn't really known for certain until now.

"I knew…from the moment…I met Jacob…that…the two of you would have a son…and that the boy would cause your…death. I couldn't let that happen. I still can't. I've…talked to the judge who gave me custody of…Jon-Jon. You will be…allowed to see him as you are now…but you can never be a mother to him."

What was she saying? That she couldn't now have custody of her son? Mama's words sliced through her. Lydia needed comfort in those dying words, not daggers. "I can't have custody?" she whimpered into the back of her mother's hands.

"Jacob will have...custody. He'll give you...supervised visits."

"Jacob? Mama, Jacob doesn't even know his son! He hasn't seen Jon since he was born. I-I don't even know where is."

"I...do. He works for a bank. A...rising star there. He's seen his son...every weekend for...the past five...years. Jacob has agreed. We've...signed papers. Upon my death, he ...gets custody of Jon-Jon."

Lydia felt her heart lift from the mire. "You're giving Jacob custody?" Oh, Goddess, the answer to her prayers! And Jacob? Was he all right? Was he happy? Was he *married?*

"I've taken...care of that...too," Mama rasped, reading her mind. "Custody is contingent on...one thing: you can never be...Jonathon's mother. You and Jacob Colter can never...marry."

Lydia stared at her mother's strained face. It was almost as if the pronouncement hurt Mama just as much as it hurt Lydia. She seemed to take in the pain straight from Lydia's heart.

Mama fingered the photo of Jon. *The binding.* She spoke more strongly now and the pain in her eyes dimmed. The life force in her radiated suddenly. "I've driven a wedge between you and your son. He will never accept your spirituality or your magick. He will...side with his father and turn away from it."

Lydia gaped. "Why, Mama? *Why?*" Why would Mama damn her and everything she loved with a dying curse?

"Because I love you too much to let you die. And if this boy lives, that is...your destiny. To die for him. And his destiny is too...important to the world."

"Don't do this. Mama, don't do this."

Mama coughed. It rattled in her throat. "Haven't much time left. I can already see the wheat fields of the Summerlands. The Goddess is calling me home." She stared at the moon through the eastern window. "Some bindings come undone when the witch that does the binding passes on. Not mine. Mine...is imbued with all the life I have left in me. It will last for all Jonathon's life...or until a witch stronger than me comes along."

Hot tears streamed down Lydia's face. This was too much. Too much. To lose Jon forever like this!

"I bind you, Jonathon Colter," Mama repeated strongly at first, then fading to a whisper. She didn't take her eyes off the waning witch moon.

"I bind you, Jonathon Colter,
From accepting your mother's magick.
I do this out of love for her and thee.
As I will it, so mote it be.
"I bind you, Jonathon Colter,
From accepting your mother's magick.
I do this...out of...love...."

The claw-like hands went limp. Breath ceased to move the feeble chest. A rush of energy sizzled through the room and drifted above and away.

Lydia lifted her watering eyes to the ceiling and screamed until she was hoarse.

Chapter Six

Early Spring, 1981
Somewhere in the Blue Ridge Mountains

Jacob's best guess was that they were somewhere in Eastern Tennessee or Western North Carolina. The only road signs they'd seen for the past ten miles warned of 5 miles per hour speed limits, sharp curves, and sharper inclines. Since they'd stopped in a hole-in-the-road town called Lingering Shade and bought a sack of groceries for an eventual picnic, he and Lydia hadn't seen another car. Good thing, too, because the narrow, hair-pin road through the mountains didn't allow room for two cars at once.

Taking the scenic route was a mistake, obviously. The

moving van would surely beat them to their new home in Washington, D.C. He wasn't sure now why he'd suggested the detour, except that Lydia had been so sad lately. He had to admit he was disappointed. They were together now, the three of them. Jacob, Lydia, and their little boy. A family. Even if he couldn't marry Lydia. Even if Lydia didn't officially have a right to Jon. They were together, and that's what mattered. And if they were together, he could find a way to take away Lydia's sadness.

"What are you thinking?" he asked, hands gingerly on the steering wheel.

Lydia didn't seem to hear. She sat no more than three feet away, but she might as well have been on another planet or years into the future. Maybe she was nervous about the new job. This move was a big step for them both. Lydia had signed on with a well-respected environmental law firm. The salary had been surprisingly good, and Jacob was pleased with that, even though the firm's clients tended to be a little too radical, too political, for his Republican tastes.

Jacob himself had taken a more conservative route. He'd finished his MBA and accepted a position as a financial strategist at a major bank in the Capitol. His reputation as a financial whiz kid had spread, and though he'd had more lucrative offers in Chicago and New York City, he'd chosen a promising position in a city that offered Lydia more opportunities. His choice had been a small sacrifice to make. The two of them still had plenty to work out from the lost years they'd been apart.

"What are you thinking?" he tried again.

Lydia stared out at the road ahead. The single-lane death trap had been carved into the side of the mountain, with a rock wall to their right and a deep canyon to their left.

He turned down the radio. "Are you worried about finding a good kindergarten in D.C.?"

"Huh? Oh." She shook herself. "Sorry. I was lost in that song."

"Oh." He could have kicked himself. Rod Stewart's "Tonight's the Night" ended on a sexy note and a plaintive memory. The song hadn't fazed Jacob, but Lydia had a weird sense of recall and never forgot anything. "You're thinking about the first night we were together again? The night your mother died?" The night they'd made tender love for the first time in years. She'd waited all those years for him, just as he'd waited for her.

Lydia nodded, but only once. "We have so much time to make up." She wrung her hands.

He reached across the seat and squeezed her thigh. "Don't be so nervous. This is all going to work out. High-powered jobs, a great apartment, our little Jon-Jon. We're going to have a great life, Lydia." He lifted her hand to his lips and brushed the smoothness of her skin.

"I just want to...."

"What? Get there? Get started on our life together? I know."

"To get out of these mountains."

"Why?" He let her hand drop as he negotiated another turn. "I thought you loved the mountains. Didn't you call them the Watchtowers of Northern Earth or something like that?"

"I do like the mountains, but...." She sighed and adjusted her voluminous velvet skirt. "I have a bad feeling, that's all."

Jacob's jaw tightened. "Damn it, Lydia. Don't start that again." After all the trouble her drug-induced hallucinations had been—all her tales of witchery had cost them as a family—Lydia had had the nerve to confess that she still had visions and premonitions, even without drugs as a catalyst. A gift from the Goddess, she'd called it. Well, he didn't believe in a goddess, and if there were such a thing, the goddess had surely let her naïve worshipper suffer for nothing! He loved Lydia so much, but sometimes she could make him awfully mad. Her candles burning at midnight. Her chanting at a full moon. Her strange crescent moon headbands. If she'd only forfeit all the witchcraft mumbo-jumbo, their life would be perfect.

Tears rolled down Lydia's cheeks. "Mama was right."

Jacob swallowed the lump in his throat. He'd never developed a fondness for Mrs. Stevenson, but seeing her waste away had softened his heart. No one—not even an overprotective, manipulative bitch—deserved that kind of ending.

"Right about what?" he asked, careful not to sound too

harsh.

"The night Jon was born, she told me your lack of understanding in my Wiccan faith would bring me heartache. She was right."

He sighed, making damned sure she heard it. "If you want to be a religious fanatic, fine, but why can't you pick a real religion? Follow Jesus or Mohammed or Buddha, I don't care. Why do you always have to be so weird?"

This time it was Lydia who gritted her teeth. Her eyes flashed at him, the first time ever. God, she was pissed!

"Do not ever," she began through clenched teeth, "call me names in front of our son!" She turned to look in the backseat where Jon lay curled in a blanket. For a second, she looked relieved to find him sleeping. She turned back to Jacob and pointed her finger at him. "I will not stay with a man who shows me disrespect in front of my child."

But she would. Jacob knew it. He wouldn't say anything, but they both knew that Lydia would stay with him because he had custody of Jon. She loved her boy that much. If Jacob were an ogre and mind to mistreat her in all sorts of ways, even then she might stay with him. But he wasn't like that. He loved her. And she loved him. And if she would only give up on this "alternative religion," everything would be perfect between them. There was absolutely nothing else that they argued about—ever. Couldn't she see how important it was to him that she give it up?

"And can't you see how important it is to me that you accept me as I am? A witch?"

Jacob startled. How did she *do* that? Read his mind?

The air in the car was much too thick. Lydia would have said it was negative energy or some fool comment like that, but to him, it was simply tension. And it wasn't about to break by itself.

"Let's pull over up here at this bridge," he said. Already he was steering and braking. They were getting out for a breath of fresh air, with or without Lydia's agreement. "It's lunch time anyway. We can have a picnic and then Jon can get his feet wet in the stream."

Lydia gasped as he pulled the key out of the ignition. She stared straight ahead at the tumbling waters. Her rosy cheeks had turned ashen.

"Lydia?"

She didn't move except to let her mouth drop open a notch.

Jacob swore under his breath. "Fine. You stay in the car. Jon-Jon and I will go have a picnic without you." He slammed the door, harder than he meant. It felt good to blow off a little steam. He was certainly open to a debate on the subject of religion, but just as soon as he said the first negative word about Wicca, Lydia clammed up. Well, enough already!

"No, wait!" Lydia scrambled out the passenger door. "You can't let Jon go to the water alone. I'll—I'll go. I'll...." She let out a ragged sigh of her own. Resignation tinged her voice. "I'll get the picnic supplies out of the trunk."

Jacob nodded and exchanged a tentative glance with her. He hated to argue. If she'd only talk reasonably instead of being so damned incommunicative. "Good," he said. "I'll get Jon-Jon."

Jon was already awake in the back seat and rubbing at his eyes. He clutched a flannel blanket of moons and stars in one hand and a paperback book in the other. *The Temple of the Twelve* by Esmerelda Little Flame. Jacob had heard Lydia reading the book to Jon at bedtime, and though the concepts were sometimes too deep for a six-year-old, Jon-Jon loved the mental imagery of the colors coming to life to teach spiritual lessons. Jacob didn't remember hearing about witchcraft—not once—which was what Lydia generally spent her non-lawyer time reading.

She'd just finished another book, Selene Silverwind's *Once Upon a Beltane Eve*, which Lydia said was a bit too grown-up for Jon. Still, Jon-Jon spent hours at a time staring at the unusual cover. As for Jacob, she tended to remove the book discreetly before he could figure out what the book was really about. He'd heard her read parts of it aloud, too, on nights when Jon had trouble sleeping and wanted to hear his mother's lilting voice. Sometimes she read about celebrations. Sometimes she quoted something sounding like poems. Every time Jacob walked into the room, Lydia closed the book and went mute.

Both books were beautifully written and interesting, but

they sounded more like inspirational literature than tales of witch-craft and curses. Why then did she hide them from him? He didn't understand this one corner of her life at all, and because he couldn't understand it, he wanted her to get rid of it. He had to see what secrets she hid away in her heart or help purge her of them.

Jon-Jon wrapped his scrawny little arms around his daddy's neck and let Jacob carry him down the rock-laden de-cline. They stepped from stone to stone, finally finding one large enough to set out a picnic on. Jacob set the boy down. As Jon-Jon's feet touched the ground, he asked, "Why were you and Lyddie fighting?"

Jacob inhaled. How much had the boy heard? "We weren't fighting, Jon. Your mother and I were just having a dis-cussion."

"You were fighting about me." Jon looked up at him, his mouth in a standard Lydia-pout. He had straight blond hair that curled at the ends between haircuts and huge blue eyes like Jacob's, only Jon hadn't grown into them yet.

"No," Jacob answered honestly. "We weren't fighting about you, but there is something you can do to make Lydia hap-pier." He glanced over his shoulder to see Lydia some distance behind, hauling a bag of Cokes and sandwich makings down the rocks. He whispered to Jon-Jon, "You can call Lyddie 'Mommy.'"

Jon's eyes brightened. He grinned mischievously. Mrs. Stevenson had urged him to call her "Mama" and to think of Lydia as a sister. In the six months since his grandmother's death, he'd had a really tough time. Too many changes. Thankfully, Jacob and Lydia had been in his life for years, though separately, so he didn't feel the brunt of loss as badly as he might have oth-erwise. Now he faced a new home and a new lifestyle.

"She'll like that," Jon agreed. He crawled up on another rock and waited. "But 'Mommy' is for little kids, so from now on, I'll call her 'Mom.'"

Jacob nodded as Lydia reached their rock a good twenty feet from the stream. The water gurgled and splashed, striking the white rocks in its midst and turning to foam. Its smell was distinctive and not unpleasant, but with the cool mountain breezes at their backs, Jacob caught only an occasional whiff.

"Hi, Mom!" Jon piped up and slid off the rock, grinding some green mold into his the seat of his pants. He grinned from ear to ear. "I love you, Mom!"

Lydia set down the sack of groceries on the big rock and burst into tears. She wrapped her arms tightly around her son, tears trailing down her cheeks, and held him. She said nothing.

"Hey, kiddo." Jacob tried to lighten the mood. He gave Jon a playful slap on his mold-stained behind. "Go look for some rocks we can take to our new house with us and let your mother and me do some talking."

Jon ran off downstream. He must have known his parents were trying to get rid of him, but the prospect of rock-hunting outweighed any hard feelings.

Lydia, on the other hand, was a total wreck. Pale cheeks, tangled hair, tear-filled eyes, and full of fidgets. "Thank you," she murmured.

"For what?"

"For putting Jon up to the that."

"Up to what?" Jacob tried to play dumb, but he wasn't any good at it with Lydia. She always seemed to know what he was thinking.

She smiled through her tears, but kept her distance. "I love you, Jacob Colter. *So* much." She sniffed and wiped a tear. "I wish we could have had more time together."

"So do I. But we'll have it in D.C."

She didn't respond. A million miles away again.

"But while we're on the subject of wishes," he said, lifting a loaf of bread from the grocery sack, "I really wish we could be married."

"We are married. In my mind. We were married the night of our hand-fasting."

They were married in his mind, too, though he didn't equate it to that odd little ritual she'd performed after they'd found out she was pregnant. A pretty ritual, yes, but it didn't mean the same to him as it obviously did to her. He couldn't tell her that, but of course, she already knew.

"As far as other people are concerned," he said, "you are

Lydia *Colter.* We're moving to a new city, a new start on life, and it's the perfect time for you to take a new name."

She smiled a little. "And as far as Jon is concerned, we were married five months before he was born. And he doesn't ever have to know all the pain we've been through to be with him."

"Agreed." Jacob set two bottles of Coke and a small carton of milk on the rock. "And he doesn't ever have to know about any of that witch crap—"

A horrific look crossed her face. Lydia took off running, almost toppling him as she pushed past. She headed downstream as fast as she could. *Shit.* What had he said now?

"You just don't understand, do you?"

Jacob whirled on the voice behind him. A familiar blonde stood at the corner of the rock, close enough to touch him. Where the hell had she come from? She wore a white pantsuit—an outdated nurse's uniform—and bright blue eye shadow that made her lids look like garage doors opening and closing. Jacob's gaze riveted to the name tag: Maddie.

"You," he breathed. "Where did you come from?"

She hadn't been there a moment before. The last time he'd seen her was the night Jon was born. She'd protested Mrs. Stevenson's actions and helped him slip past two security guards so he could see his son and Lydia. What was she doing out in the middle of nowhere, looking exactly—*exactly*—the same as she had six years ago?

"It doesn't matter. What does matter is respect and understanding."

"Wh-what?"

"You want Lydia to give up her spirituality. She can no more give it up than she can give up her son."

Jacob took a step backward. He gestured wildly, accidentally knocking a Coke from the rock. The bottle shattered and foamed on a rock at his feet. "What—what business is any of this to you?"

He felt guilty, speaking so harshly to the nurse. He owed her more than she could imagine.

"Elisha, you've got to try to—"

"What did you call me?" Jacob backed up another step. He kept his distance. Elisha was his middle name, a name he didn't use.

She shrugged and moved a step closer. "That's your name, isn't it? Jacob Elisha Colter."

"How did you—"

"It's not important." She waved away his questions. "You don't understand Lydia's religion. A shame, that. The two of you working together could be very powerful. Blessed."

"Lydia doesn't have a religion." Why was he even bothering to talk to this woman? Except that she'd done a good turn for him the night Jon was born? Except she'd appeared out of thin air at exactly the spot where he'd spontaneously decided to stop for a picnic?

"You're telling me you haven't noticed Lydia's religion?"

"Oh. The witchcrap. Look, that's not a religion. Just ask anybody."

"No? Just ask anybody, then. Anybody who practices it." Maddie frowned at him and closed the gap. She laid a warm hand on his shoulder. "Do you even know what it is she believes?"

"N-no." He stumbled and caught himself. "I don't need to know."

"Are you sure? All you want to do is debate spirituality, not experience it. And every time you put down what she believes, she so strongly identifies with her spirituality that she feels you're putting her down, too. Then she walls herself off from you to keep from feeling hurt."

"How would you know—"

"Listen. I don't have much time. I know you love Lydia. But if you're to have a life with her, you must accept that she and her religion are a package deal. Understand what she understands—that every living thing has a spirit, that we're all connected and all part of the same Universe, that she finds Deity in Nature rather than in stained-glass windows and pewter offering plates, that she finds what others call God not outside and away in heaven, but inside and close. Ask her about these things, Elisha, and listen with an open mind. If you don't, you'll lose her."

Jacob shook his head. "I don't believe in mumbo-jumbo, and I don't like having a stranger pop up out of nowhere to tell me how to live my life. If I can't see it, why should I believe in something no one can prove is there?"

"Sometimes, Elisha, you have to have faith. Belief in that which cannot be seen or heard by those not willing to see or to listen. But if you need proof, I'll give it to you now. Your wife will die today—"

"What?" he interrupted. His heart skipped a beat. Even if this woman was just making up something to scare him, the thought of it gnawed at him.

"Your wife will die today," she continued, "unless you go to her *now*."

"Yeah, right."

"It is never wise to tamper with someone else's fate without permission, but you can change your own future. You can never change your past. And the future, unchanged, quickly becomes past. What will it be, Elisha? Will you raise my sweet Jonathon alone? I'll leave it up to you. For now, I've done all *I* can."

He blinked, and she was gone. A gold shimmer hung in the air and dissipated. A sizzle faded. No human being could do what Maddie had done. Not unless—

"Your wife will die today unless you go to her now."

"Lydia!" he screamed. He hopped from rock to rock, slipping and sliding on the damp surfaces. "Lydia!"

He ran headlong down the mountain, eyes trained on the stream and woods. *Where is she?*

Then he saw it. Jon-Jon crying, clawing at a pointed rock in the middle of the rumbling stream. Somehow he managed to stay above water, but just barely. Something—a stick or small limb—had caught his belt and held it up.

The sun shifted on the water and Jacob knew then. Lydia. Lydia, from beneath the surface, pushed a pole up under Jon's narrow belt and held him up while the last of her breath bubbled out of her. Jon grabbed the top of the rock and held on.

"Lydia!" Jacob sailed into the water. The current was stronger than expected. It tugged at his feet. It slammed him against the rocks. The impact jarred the breath from his lungs, and he nearly went under.

He reached Jon first, giving him a quick push up onto the rock, to more permanent safety. Then Jacob pulled Lydia up for air. Her skirts ballooned with water, weighed her down, tangled in the brush, trapped her against the rocks. Holding his breath, Jacob fumbled with the fabric, tore at it to loosen the skirt. Finally, he ripped it, freeing her. He dragged her back to the surface and then snared Jon with his free hand. He half-walked, half-carried them to the bank of the stream.

The three of them lay there on the spring grass—coughing and sputtering but alive.

"I made it," Lydia said, panting. She shuddered from an uncontrollable chill. "I made it. I wasn't supposed to."

Jacob gathered her into his arms and pressed her cheek into his wet shoulder. He stroked Jon's soggy curls with the other hand. No. No, Lydia wasn't supposed to make it, according to Maddie. A stranger had given him a second chance to be a dad and a husband, to have a future with the woman he loved. Without that stranger, he would never have found Lydia—and maybe not Jon-Jon—until it was too late. For that he would always be grateful.

Then he remembered what Maddie had said years ago in that hospital corridor:

"I'm a good friend of Jonathon's."

Chapter Seven

Early afternoon in the Spring of 1988
Jacob and Lydia's home in the Chicago suburbs

Lydia stood at the door to Jon's room and peered through the crack. She should have been fuming, but the kid was so damned cute. He was all of thirteen, gangly and full of mischief. His blond hair skimmed his shoulders and flew all around his head as he bounced around on his bed, playing air guitar and singing at the top of his lungs.

"Haht lay-igs!"

Lydia stifled a laugh. The boy had always had a fondness for Rod Stewart songs, but Jon's rendition of "Hot Legs" would have been enough to make the singer resign at once.

Jon sprawled out one leg and angled his butt in the opposite direction. "I love yah, hunnnneeeee!"

Lydia put on her sternest face and shoved the door open. "Jonathon Colter!"

He froze, air guitar in mid-strum. He no longer bounced on the bed, but the mattress springs still quivered. His eyes grew to the size of saucers. "Uh...Mom! What are *you* doing home?"

"I might ask you the same thing, young man." She folded her arms in front of her. She'd been half-way through her research into a hazardous waste dumping incident at work when she'd seen a quick flash of Jon in the principal's office. "School's not out for another two hours."

"I...um...they...er...."

She almost felt sorry for him. He didn't stand a chance. "You got sent home for cutting up in the lunch room, didn't you?"

He looked crushed. Jon slid down from the bed. "Mrs. Isyet called you? She promised not to call you and worry you at work. She said I just had to take my punishment and then I could go home for the day. She said she wouldn't call you." He glared up at Lydia. "She lied."

"She didn't call me."

"Then how did you—?" Realization lit his face. "Aw, MMMMMommmmmmmm!"

How he could turn one syllable into five was beyond her grasp, but Lydia confirmed his suspicions with a nod. "You're grounded, buster. No TV for two weeks."

"I'll miss 'Cheers' and 'Night Court'!"

"Wanna try for three weeks?"

Jon flopped onto the bed and crossed his arms. "It's so unfair!"

"Life is full of unfair. Just because you got into trouble at school and sweet-talked your principal out of calling me does not mean you're not in trouble at home."

"Argh!" He rolled onto his back and stared up at the ceiling. "Why can't you be a normal mom?" he wailed.

Lydia caught her breath. "What's that supposed to mean?"

"All my friends have normal moms. You're, like, always in my head. It's invasion of privacy—that's what it is! I can't do anything without you knowing. I hate the way you use witchcraft to find things out about me. Why don't you just ask?"

Lydia stared at him. He'd never spoken to her with such acidity. Ever. He was on the verge of his teen years and their accompanying monstrosity, but she hadn't expected ugliness. Her eyes stung. Jon had sided with his father against her magick. Her mother's binding still held.

And then…she was some place else. A darkened school corridor. Shiny floor. A row of lockers. Hands spinning a combination lock and opening a battered gray locker. Something in a brown paper bag. The bag inside the locker. The locker unlocked, slightly open. The row of gray lockers in the hall. The hall quiet and waiting. A clock on the wall. Black rim with white face. Oversized numbers. Two o'clock. The bell rang. Loud, ear-splitting. Students spilling into the corridors, past the lockers, some of the kids stopping to exchange textbooks. Then orange. A flash of orange…then blood on the freshly waxed floors.

"Mom? Mom, I didn't mean it! I'm sorry. Mom?

Jon was on the floor in front of her. Somehow, she'd fallen to the carpet. She clung to the wall.

Jon. He was all right. Safe. He was home. Home at—she glanced at the clock on the wall—one-thirty in the afternoon.

Lydia scrambled to her feet. What she'd seen hadn't happened yet. It could be stopped. She'd realized seven years ago at a mountain stream that visions weren't always mandatory previews of things that couldn't be changed. They were sometimes warnings. Opportunities to change the future. Jon was alive today because she'd seen in her mind's eye when he'd crossed the stream and fallen into the rushing waters. She'd reached him just in time to see it happen.

"Mom! Mom, what's wrong? I didn't mean to hurt your feelings. I didn't mean it!" Jon himself was close to crying.

Lydia stumbled into the kitchen and seized the phone.

She punched in the telephone number for the principal at Jon's junior high school—Lydia knew it from memory.

"There's a bomb," she said breathlessly into the phone. "You've got to get the kids out of there—*now!*"

"Would you hold a moment for the principal?" a receptionist's voice asked.

It seemed forever before someone picked up the phone. "Hello? Who is this?"

Lydia could hear a loud bell in the background. Good. Already, they were evacuating. "Mrs. Isyet?"

"Yes. Who's calling?"

"There's a bomb in the east wing. It's set to go off at two o'clock. Get out now!"

"What makes you think there's a bomb in our school?" Mrs. Isyet was trying to be calm, but Lydia could hear the edge in her voice. Lydia had had enough face-to-face meetings with her about Jon's antics that she felt as if she knew the woman as a friend.

"Damn it, Pauline! This is Lydia Colter. Now drop the phone and get out of there now or there are going to be dead people everywhere, you included!"

Less than an hour after the principal dropped the phone and ran, a dozen police cars with flashing blue lights showed up at Lydia's door.

Chapter Eight

A huge full moon hung on the horizon. One edge had started to fade away.

Jacob slammed the car in park and eased out the driver's door. He'd been driving for a solid seven hours. Tension in his shoulders and neck exploded in a headache. He was exhausted, confused, angry.

He had been away on a business trip, in the middle of perhaps the most important meeting of his banking career, when a nervous secretary had interrupted to announce that his son was on the line. Another argument with his mother, Jacob had assumed. When he heard Jon's voice, he knew it was more than that.

Jon had tried to sound brave, but the shaky voice was a dead giveaway. "Dad, you've got to come home. Now," Jon had urged. "Mom's been arrested for blowing up my school."

Jacob might have thought it was a joke, except that, with Lydia, anything was possible. He'd walked out on his vital meeting and dashed straight to the airport to catch a flight home. An afternoon fog had descended on the airport, however, so Jacob had rented a car and hit the road. Mud still dripped from the flaps behind the tires as Jacob banged the door shut and headed for the police station doors.

After twenty heated minutes, one of the officers escorted Jacob to an interrogation room. Jon met him at the door with a desperate hug.

"Where's your mother?" Jacob asked, once he was certain Jon was okay. He ignored the pug-faced detective seated at the table.

"They're still grilling her, Dad."

"Questioning her," the detective corrected.

Jon cast a chilling glare at the man. "*Grilling* her, Dad. She's been in there since three o'clock this afternoon. They won't let me see her. Dad," he wailed, "they think she planted a bomb in my school!"

Jacob matched Jon's glare at the detective. "My wife would never do anything as stupid as that. We're a peace-loving family. We don't believe in bombs and violence. And what are you doing questioning my son without a lawyer present? Or *me*?"

The detective shrugged. "Your son volunteered."

"He's a kid. You'll lead him on and turn his words against my wife." Jacob caught his breath. Since when had he become so cynical? He'd always believed in the system, but Lydia blowing up kids? This was ridiculous. How could he trust a system that made this kind of mistake? "I need some time alone with my son, if you don't mind." The detective shrugged again and left the room. Jacob turned back to Jon. "Now tell me everything. Where did they get the crazy idea your mom made a bomb threat?"

"I was there, Dad. She called Mrs. Isyet and told her

there was a bomb in one of the lockers."

"What? Why would she do that?"

"I dunno. She was being weird again." Jon perched on the corner of the table and swung his legs. "I know it looks bad, Dad, but she didn't do any of the things they said." Jon knitted his eyebrows in the direction of the two-way mirror behind Jacob. Someone was watching him—both of them—and Jon's angry expression was meant to let the detectives outside know that he knew he was being watched.

"What makes everything so suspicious," Jon continued, "is that she wasn't at work when the bomb was planted. And I wasn't in school."

"Why the hell not?"

"Got in trouble in the lunch room and got sent home," Jon mumbled. "Mom came home from work early and found me there."

Jacob sighed. It seemed lately that Jon was always in some kind of minor trouble at school. A phase, he hoped. Jon was sometimes a little too impulsive and too eager to defy authority. But that could wait. "Why did she come home from work early? Your principal called her again, didn't she?"

"Nope. Mom had one of those feelings—again. Knew all about me screwing up. Dad, I hate it when she does that!"

Jacob rubbed his son's bony shoulder. "So do I, Jon. So do I."

He'd tried to understand Lydia's visions after that day at the stream when he'd nearly lost her. He'd even done as Maddie had suggested and asked her about her religion, but no matter how hard he tried, he just couldn't understand it. He's never had a vision. In fact, he didn't even dream much. But regardless of how much he loved her, he was bone-weary of Lydia's beliefs.

"Dad, she had another feeling or daydream or something. She ran to the phone and called Mrs. Isyet and told her to evacuate. She told them her name. Dad, people who make bomb threats don't give their names out. Can't those stupid detectives see that?" Again, he scrunched his face at the two-way mirror in defiance.

"It's all right, son. Your mother may be a little nuts, but

she wouldn't hurt a fly." Or anything other living thing. That much of her beliefs he'd understood.

Jon set his lips in that perfect Lydia-pout. "Then I guess I'm glad she's a little nuts, 'cause there really was a bomb and it really did go off. If Mom hadn't called the school to tell them, almost two hundred kids could have been hurt or killed."

They sat in silence for a long time, Jon lost in his own world and Jacob wishing for a normal life. Nothing had ever been normal with Lydia. No doubt, the detectives knew by now that she didn't have custody of Jon and that he, Jacob, was not her husband, legally. There was no sane reason for what Lydia had done today, and cops tended to look for the obvious reasons. Lydia had lost custody of her son and wasn't married to his father. Lydia openly wore a pentagram-shaped pendant on a silver necklace. Lydia had fled work early and with no explanation. Her son had been sent home from school at the same time. Her son had been in trouble too often this academic year. Her son wasn't at school when the bomb was set to go off. She identified herself when she made the "threat." She made the "threat" from her home telephone. She had motive and opportunity as well as distinct knowledge of the crime. Voila! Guilty. Case closed.

If he knew Lydia, she had waived having a lawyer present for questioning and had told them open and honestly everything she had seen in her visions. She believed in the truth, damn the consequences of it. Jacob sighed. Lydia was doomed.

The door to the interrogation room opened. The pug-faced detective stepped inside, looking perplexed. "Mr. Colter? You can see Lydia Stevenson now. You can take her home if you'd like."

"Stevenson?" Jon asked. "Who's Lydia Stevenson?"

Jacob shushed him. "Just like that? You're letting her go?"

The detective nodded. "The kid who planted the bomb just turned himself in."

"What?" Jacob and Jon said in unison.

"Kid got expelled last week for carrying a gun to school. Decided to get even, so he enlisted his big brother's help to make a bomb."

Jon made a face. "I know the kid you're talking about. Thinks he's so cool. He would never turn himself in."

The detective shook his head. "Probably not, but some nurse hauled him in by his ear—literally. The kid was scared to death." He laughed. "Kid pissed all over himself while he was spilling his guts. I love it when they do that." He raised an eyebrow at Jon as if he'd expected the same of an alleged mad bomber's son.

"You said a nurse brought him in?" The hair stood up on the back of Jacob's neck. *Maddie.* He ran to the door and opened it wide. "Where is she now?"

The detective scratched his head. "We have no idea."

Chapter Nine

Magick burned in her hands. Lydia folded it into a ball and hurled it into the soil at her feet. There. It was done. She'd grounded and given the energy of her circle back to the Earth.

Lydia sank down onto the cool grass where she'd cast a circle in her back yard and lifted her gaze to the night skies. A few of the brighter stars shimmered, but the light of the waning full moon cast a veil of light over them and faded their power. Here at midnight, the moon was almost at the top of the heavens.

Jacob had fallen asleep not long ago, exhausted from his emergency road trip home. Jon, on the rim of his adolescent rage of hormones, had turned out the light in his room but was probably still awake, contemplating the day and trying to make sense of some of the things he'd heard about a woman called Lydia Stevenson. It wasn't every day that your mom's warning of a bomb was mistaken for a death threat. The kids at school would probably tease him mercilessly if they found out. And it wasn't every day you came so dangerously close to finding out your mother's darkest secrets.

But Jacob. Oh, Jacob. He hadn't said a word since he'd brought her home. She knew why. The visions. The embarrassment of having a wife who was somewhere between eccentric and totally nuts. He never mentioned it, but she knew he'd been passed over for promotions at other jobs because of her. She didn't fit the mold of the polite, church-going socialite of a banker's wife. She preferred laying Tarot cards to the cocktail party meet-and-greets Jacob always needed to attend. Too often, she blamed her work as a lawyer and begged off so that Jacob attended the official functions alone. Better that than have them find out how "different" she was.

She'd been fortunate in her own career. Mama had probably blessed her somehow, but the law firms all seemed to love Lydia's creativity and unusual style. They rewarded her with some of their hardest projects, though more and more as a researcher and less as a courtroom lawyer. She'd saved the day more than once, and for that her current law firm had been quite grateful. Unfortunately, the promotions went to less creative, more conservative employees she herself had trained. Yes, they loved her style, but it wasn't what they preferred in management positions.

And she could accept that. It hurt, but she could accept it.

What she couldn't accept was Jacob's silence. If only he believed. If only he understood. She wanted more than anything to share with him how it felt to perform magick. The warmth and energy in her fingertips. The sense of the Goddess filling her at her esbat, or full moon, rituals. The vibrations of stones and herbs sending out their essences, their spirit, to all who would accept their gifts. The connectedness she felt with all living things and all things of Earth and Sea and Heaven and Fire. Or just someone to listen when she needed to talk about her visions.

That's why she'd performed a ritual to make him understand.

"You should never have done that."

Lydia jumped to her feet. "Who's there?" She searched the dimness around her and gasped. A woman in white stood in the shadows of the hedge. Her pantsuit gleamed in the moonlight. "Oh, Goddess...."

"No. Just Her servant."

"Jon told me what happened at the police station. The nurse who brought in the real culprit. That was you, wasn't it?"

Lydia didn't need to ask. She'd seen it. Maddie stepping out of a vanishing ball of flame right before the young teen's eyes. He'd wet his pants, screamed, begged—in that order. He'd thought she was an angel of retribution, and he was right. She'd promised to carry him to hell if he failed to confess at once. The court's punishment for building and setting a bomb was nothing by comparison, and he'd gladly babbled the truth to the first officer he saw.

"I suppose I should thank you," Lydia said, bowing her head.

"You already have. Back in December of 1999."

Lydia slanted a good look at Maddie. *The Falconer. The High Priestess of the Remnants. Lorelei.* She hadn't changed at all since Lydia last saw her eight years ago. In fact, she hadn't changed in the thirteen years since Jon was born. Same hair style, same eye shadow, same white nurse's uniform. Nor had she aged. On the night of Jon's birth, Maddie had seemed a few years older than Lydia. At the Cancer Ward, the night Mama died, Maddie had seemed young, closer to Lydia's age. Now, Lydia could tell she was older than Maddie—or at least looked it—by several years.

Lydia nodded to herself. Not only did she know who *Lorelei* was, but Lydia knew *what* she was. Lydia had seen that, too. The gate of fire. *Enoch's Gate.* Where science, myth, and magick united to form a gate between worlds and between times. A gate to changing the future...from the past. Lydia had seen Lorelei in the future take a gate to the past to take a gate to the present. She'd heard Lorelei call the Watchtower Guardians, who also guarded the Gates of Heaven, foretold in the neglected *Book of Enoch.*

"I know who you are," she said simply.

Maddie nodded. "Your oldest friend. As you are mine."

Lydia could barely hear her for the rushing of her own pulse. There was so much she wanted to say, to know. "Why have you been gone so long? I've missed our talks."

"We'll have more time in the future."

"In your future or mine?"

Maddie smiled. "You *do* understand. In your future, my

past. Jon will need you then, need your special abilities. We both will need you. You *and* Jacob."

Lydia sighed. So much she wanted to know, but none of it was truly important. She and Jacob and Jon all had a future together. What more could someone who had seen the future say of any importance?

"There is something you must undo," Maddie said. "The spell you cast tonight. It cannot stand. You must break it. Tonight."

Lydia groaned. Maddie wanted Lydia to undo her magick when it was for such a good cause? "No! No, I can't do that."

"Lydia, it's wrong."

"Wrong? No! How could it be wrong? Don't you understand how much I want Jacob to accept what I believe? All I asked was that he come to understand my visions. What harm can come of that?"

"More than you think."

"As the moon wanes, so shall his resistance to my beliefs. It's a simple and quick working. By the time dark moon comes in two weeks, he'll appreciate the hell these visions have caused me. He'll be willing to learn about Wicca and the Goddess and the Green Man and the Craft of the Wise. He'll be more likely to look for a spiritual path, maybe even to share mine. What could be wrong with that?"

"Ask your mother."

Lydia grew still. A shiver wound its way down her spine. "What's Mama got to do with this?"

"You cannot make someone love you. He has to come to you of his own free will. And Jacob has. In spite of your differences. By the same token, you cannot make someone love your Goddess. He has to come to Her of his own free will. And Jacob won't."

"But I'll make him see—"

"That's my point. You'll *make him* see. You, by use of your magick, will alter his life's course, just as your mother altered yours to save your life. And paid the price."

A chill descended over Lydia like a fog at dusk. "But it's for a positive outcome."

"*Your* definition of positive. Lydia, he doesn't want this. He doesn't choose it freely. If you make him accept your visions, you are forcing yourself on him. It's rape by magick. You're tampering with his life's course, with something the two of you ordained before you were born. It's unethical, and you know it."

Deep down, she knew. Instead of accepting it, she shook it off. "I won't undo the spell. If Jacob will only believe in my visions and understand what it is I've seen, he and I can be *really* together. In every way that counts."

"The Rule of Three, Lydia. Have you forgotten? Whatever you send out, good or bane, will come back to you three times as powerfully."

"I can live with it."

Maddie's eyes narrowed. "Can you? Your mother knew the Rule of Three. She chose to break it and pay the consequences. Will you do the same?"

Lydia said nothing. At that moment, the most important thing in the world was having Jacob, her husband and lover, understand her and accept her, weirdness and all.

Chapter Ten

Two weeks later, day of the dark moon
Illinois countryside, dirt road

The last thing Jacob wanted to do was hurt Lydia's feelings, but something had to give. He hadn't had a decent night's sleep in the past week and a half. She'd bought a new cookbook from Jon's classroom fundraiser and had spent most of the past two weeks experimenting with new recipes. Probably some new spice or herb she'd found at one of those witch shops. Well, something in her cooking wasn't treating him right because it kept him up half the night with some of the most god-awful nightmares. By now he was so sleep-deprived that he was seeing things in broad daylight.

"So what are we doing out here in the countryside?" Lydia

asked cheerfully.

Too cheerfully. He wished she'd take over and drive so that he could sleep, but the trip had been his idea. They needed a getaway, just the two of them, while Jon stayed over at his best friend's house now that he was off restriction. They needed time alone to talk. Life in their household had been tense since the night of the alleged bomb threat. Maybe some time away—alone—would help.

"I thought you liked countryside."

"I do. *You* don't."

He shrugged, half because he didn't know how to answer and half to buck off the mantle of sleep that threatened. He gripped the steering wheel. "We needed time alone, and Jon's punishment was over, so...why not a romantic weekend at a bed and breakfast in the middle of nowhere?"

She smiled beside him. Sweet and secretive. She was happy, more so than he remembered in a long time. She scooted close and lay her head on his shoulder, nodding her contentment.

They whizzed past an empty field of farm equipment left for auction. Jacob had been there last week with one of his banking colleagues. The farmer had spent a fortune on irrigation equipment, but still the crops died awaiting rain. The rains had come eventually. Too little, too late. And the expense of running the equipment had bankrupted the man and his two sons. They'd been left with nothing, disenchanted with the Government after a federal loan program had refused to lend them money without an outrageously expensive irrigation system in place. They'd complied, borrowed more money than they could ever pay back under less than perfect circumstances, and lost everything.

At the auction, farmers had come from all around. Not to buy but to commiserate. They shook hands and talked in whispers. One man asked if he were ready for the coming revolution when common people tired of taxes and hard work would rise up. Very little had been sold that day and most of the equipment remained in the field, lined up for passersby to inspect. But Jacob had learned a wealth of information about farmers who bound machine guns in oily rags, sealed them in PVC pipe, and buried their revolution quietly beneath the waiting black soil.

He dreamed of that soil in the nights since. He saw young men and women in long-sleeved shirts, khaki pants, and boots. He saw the weapons in their grip as they stood guard against something in the night. He saw them turning farms into fortresses. They called themselves colonists, but others, elsewhere, referred to them as Remnants.

He dreamed of other things, too. Of a strange field of TV antennae in a cold field somewhere far north. Alaska, maybe. He saw a man who looked like himself and the nurse—Maddie—arguing over how to destroy the array of metal trees.

He had nightmares of walking through city streets. People lay dead where they'd fallen. Dogs, too. He unhooked the top button of his shirt and tugged his T-shirt collar over his mouth and nose to diminish the stench. He could feel dozens of pairs of eyes hiding behind broken windows.

"Jacob!"

Lydia screamed as the car plunged toward a shallow ditch. He braked, but too late. The car bumped roughly over a barbed wire fence and lurched sideways. Everything stopped—quickly.

Jacob sat in silence, trying to decide if he'd been hurt or not. He'd been dreaming. He was so tired. He must have fallen asleep. He squinted into the rear-view mirror at the for-auction equipment in the field behind them. If he'd been asleep, he hadn't been asleep for long.

"Are you…are you okay?" his passenger asked.

His attention riveted to Lydia. Yes, he was with Lydia. He'd forgotten somehow. Lost touch with reality. He'd been some place else, some place without Lydia.

He nodded slowly. "Yeah, I'm fine. You're…you're okay, too?"

"A little shook up, I guess, but all right." Her arms were still braced against the dashboard of the car. "But you're bleeding."

Bleeding? *Oh, yeah.* His head hurt like all get-out. He touched the spot on his forehead, right in the middle, above his nose. *Your third eye,* he heard Lydia say in his mind. Jacob stared at the blood on his fingertips.

"It's just a bump," Lydia said, "but we should stop at the

next town and get it looked at."

"Car's wrecked."

"The car's in better shape than you are."

She was right. The engine still ran. They were in a ditch and would need help getting out, but the car itself was fine except for a bent-in fender and perhaps a bashed headlight.

Jacob turned off the ignition and handed Lydia the key. "I think you should drive. I'm...dreaming."

Lydia gasped. "Really?" She sounded...*happy*? "What about?"

"Umph. Nightmares. I'm too tired, I guess. That and this bump on my head. Maybe I'm not doing so well after all." He fished a tissue out of the glove box and pressed its thin layers against his forehead. "We're not too far from the state line. The Mississippi River should be right over there...."

"What's wrong?"

Jacob blinked. Somehow he was sitting in the middle of a huge lake emptying into a river. He could barely see the land on either side. Somehow the Great Lakes had merged and opened up into the Mississippi River, splitting the country in half. He rubbed his eyes. His head hurt, but not so much from the bump as from the flashes of...of *visions*.

"Jacob! What's wrong?" Lydia was close to him now, taking the tissue from him and pressing it against his head. "Jacob, can you hear me?"

He nodded. "I think I have a brain injury or something. I'm-I'm seeing things. Terrible things."

She sighed her relief. Smiling, she kissed his cheek. "It's okay, Jacob. You're seeing the things I see all the time. Visions of things that happened in previous incarnations. Prophecy of what's yet to come, unless we stop it."

"Wh-what are you talking about?" He shut his eyes to block out the images of soldiers and wars.

"They'll go away after today. I promise."

He shook his head hard enough loosen the dreams, but they clung to his mind. "You don't know that. I've got to get to a doctor. You've got to go for help." He gripped his temples in both palms. He gritted his teeth. He didn't want to see any more.

"You'll be all right, Jacob. Tonight's the worst of it. Things are revealed on dark moon nights—"

His voice rose three octaves. "What the hell are you talking about?"

"I performed a spell for you, Jacob."

"Spell...?"

"A harmless one. Just one that would let you see the visions I see and—"

He stared at her. "You put a spell on me?" He shoved her away. "What kind of weirdo are you?"

That stopped her. Lydia went white. Her hands flopped to her side. "It was just through tonight. Just so you'd understand me better."

War and fire and famine and plague and Jon and running and daggers and falcons and Lorelei—

"Get away from me!" he screeched. "Get away from me!" He fumbled with the door but couldn't open it. He squeezed his eyes shut again. "I just want it to stop," he wailed.

Lydia whimpered. "I know. Being psychic can be scary, but after a while, you learn to use the visions to change the future. You have to—"

He grabbed Lydia by the wrist and yanked her to him. "I don't give a damn about using visions to change anything. I just want them to stop. May them stop, Lydia! How could you love me and curse me like this?"

"Let me go. I-I'll get help."

She sniffled and broke free. She scrambled out the passenger door and ran barefoot into the freshly plowed fields. She pointed at the ground and spun in a circle. A bluish, purplish veil of light seemed to hang in the air around her.

Jacob heard her chanting, facing each direction and calling to some kind of guardians. Then an invitation to someone or something. Then another chant as she raised her arms to the darkening skies. Somewhere was prayer of gratitude, then another circle of thanks as she faced each direction. Then, one last time, she spun around, collecting the bluish, purplish light around her in a ball in her right hand. Was he dreaming still?

She fell to the ground. He watched the light seep into the

earth. His head was clear. The bump still hurt, but the dreams and lights and visions were gone.

Jacob sighed and fell over the brink into unconsciousness.

Chapter Eleven

The next afternoon, the first night of the new moon
A small town hospital in Missouri

Lydia would never have left Jacob's bedside...if he'd let her near him.

Unable to pace, she limped around the lobby of the tiny hospital. Every time a nurse or doctor darkened the doors, she glanced up expectantly. Maybe this time, they'd let her see him. She wasn't his wife, they'd reminded her. And Mr. Colter had expressly asked *not* to see Lydia Stevenson. Whatever would she tell Jon? Whatever would she tell *herself*?

Heart aching, she sank down onto a green vinyl chair with a rip in the seat. It squawked under her weight. She was dog-tired from yesterday. After her ritual, she'd found Jacob passed out. She'd walked the lonely country road for help, at least ten miles, to the nearest farm house. The old man there had taken Jacob and Lydia to the nearest hospital fifty miles away and gone back to pull the car out of the ditch with his old Ford tractor.

A full day later, her feet still hurt so badly she could hardly walk. She had blisters on top of blisters from walking on the country road, plus a couple of deep cuts to the sole. One of the nurses had washed and bandaged her feet but her injuries weren't serious enough to warrant an overnight stay, so Lydia had spent a cramped night on one of the squeaky vinyl sofas in the hospital lobby. She hadn't had a bath all day or a change of clothes. She was miserable but far more from what was in her heart than anything physical.

Jacob doesn't want to see me.

God, that hurt. She'd loved him for as long as she could

remember, but he no longer wanted her in his life. Maddie had been right: Lydia should never have used magick to try to change Jacob's mind, especially when he felt so strongly opposed to her beliefs. She'd never felt so alone in all her life—not when she'd lost custody of Jon, not when Jacob had disappeared, not when Mama had died. Now, she felt the full brunt of the Dark Goddess—the sense of growing old and growing cold, utterly alone. Barren of heart, as winter.

Lydia buried her face in her hands and wept.

"Ms. Stevenson?"

A kindly hand shook her shoulder. She looked up to see an elderly doctor hunched over her.

"I thought you might want to know that I'm discharging Mr. Colter in the morning."

"You are?"

Oh, Jacob is all right. He's going to be okay! She sighed. *Physically.*

"Yes. I want to keep him through tonight. He needs his rest."

Poor bastard's exhausted, Lydia heard him say in his mind.

"The head injury—"

"I'll observe him for another night, but other than the bruise from where his forehead hit the steering wheel, it's all uglier than it is harmful to him."

She nodded, relieved. Even if he didn't want to be with her any longer, she was happy that he wasn't maimed for life. Not physically, at least.

"He'll see you now."

The heavy darkness lifted from Lydia's shoulders. "He will?"

The old doctor nodded. "But keep it short. I've given him a sedative to help him rest. You've got maybe five minutes before he's down for the night."

Lydia thanked him and ran for Jacob's room. He wanted to see her, and every moment was precious. He lay snuggled and calm under the soft white sheets. Someone had spread a cotton blanket over his legs and feet. Jacob stretched out, staring at the ceiling, his hands folded over his heart. He didn't look at her.

"Jacob?" She dropped to the straight chair beside his bed and pulled it close. One look at Jacob not looking at her, and she bowed her head in shame. "I should never have used magick on you. I broke my own rules. I'm so sorry, Jacob."

"It's Elisha."

"What?" She lifted her head.

Slowly, he turned his face toward her. "From now on, I choose to be known as Elisha. Because I'm a changed man."

Oh, Goddess. What had she done? She'd had visions of him in the future—visions of Elisha. A leader among men. A dangerous one.

"Jac—" She stopped herself. "Elisha. You have to know that I never meant to hurt you. All I wanted was for you to understand what it's like to have these visions I have and how they're a gift because they can be used to change the future. I thought if you could just understand that I'm not...different...on purpose, then you wouldn't be so harsh about my spirituality. I thought—"

He clasped her hand and silenced her. He held on tightly. "I know, Lydia," he said in the softest voice she'd ever heard. "I know."

She drank him in with her eyes. She wanted to remember everything about him. She had to. She didn't know why, but she had to. His soft blonde hair and light blue eyes. The curve of his chin and eyebrows. The gauze square taped over his third eye where he'd pummeled the steering wheel. No matter what he called himself, she would always love him. Always.

"I didn't like that you used your witchcraft on me, Lydia. I still don't. But I understand why." His voice was too quiet, too soft, too ethereal. Perhaps the sedative was working its own magick. "Lydia, I used to make fun of your visions. It thought it was just a wacky side of you I would always have to live with. I didn't know, Lydia." He squeezed her hand. "I didn't *know.*"

Tears brimmed in her eyes. She backhanded them with her free hand. "It's okay. It's okay."

"No. It isn't. I had no idea what you were seeing. Or what your Goddess meant to you. Or that magick was *real.* Oh, Lydia." He sighed and again stared up at the ceiling. "You've opened my eyes to something."

"You won't have any more visions." She shook her head furiously. "I ended the spell. No more visions. Or at least none caused by me."

"Doesn't matter. I've seen it." He turned his cheek back to her and strained to kiss the top of her head. "Things have to change. Today. I'll pack as soon as I'm home tomorrow."

Lydia tried to ignore the sinking feeling in the pit of her stomach. Perspiration prickled at her hairline. She felt sick. "Pack?" she managed weakly.

He nodded. His eyes watered. "Lydia...I...I have to leave you."

"No!"

"Don't make this any harder than it already is."

"No!" Lydia howled. She balled her fist and hit the mattress as hard as she could. "No! Jacob, don't do this! We're a family. You can't do this."

"It doesn't mean I don't love you." He snared her hand and held it until she stilled. "It's because I love you and Jon."

"You're still angry at me about the spell—"

"No, I'm not angry. But yes, it is because of the spell. Because of the visions. I've seen the future. Mine, yours, Jon's. And we are not together. Not if we all do what we have to do."

"Jacob—"

"Shhh. Listen, Lydia. You have to quit your job. Take Jon and go to California. You'll be needed there for another twelve years—but don't stay any longer than that. You'll need to leave before the oceans shift. You gave up your calling for me, and you have to get it back."

She shook her head. "I haven't given up any kind of calling. If anything, it's you who gave up your chance at a glorious career because I couldn't fit in with your conservative lifestyle."

"Then you abandoned your calling and didn't know it. You should have been teaching others of the way of the Goddess. You should have been using your visions and hypnosis to ease the pain of those around you. When you left your mother's coven to be with me, you postponed your destiny."

Jacob blinked at her through sleepy lids. The sedative

was starting to drift away with him.

"Lydia, I've seen you in the future. You'll study hypno-therapy and lecture with teaching covens. You'll be very famous, even though you won't want it. You'll lead 144,000 of your fol-lowers—healers and craftsmen—into the mountains where you'll be safe from changes in our planet. And Lydia, you will be there to save our son."

She raked in a sob. He was talking of wondrous things and horrific things. She herself had seen them all and denied so many of them.

"I will not be with you in the mountains, Lydia. I have a different destiny. Those farmers I talked to last week? I've seen myself with them in the future. Teaching militia groups. Pro-tecting the farmland and ranches. Don't you see? We both have places we have to be to do what must be done to save our world after the pole shift. Your healers and my warriors will re-unite what's left of this country—the Remnants of Humanity—and it will be Jon and...and this woman named Lorelei who will lead them."

Lydia stared at him. Yes. She'd seen it, too. One pos-sible future. "There are many possible futures."

"But that's the way it *must* happen. Any other way and we all die. Everyone. Every person on the face of our planet." His words began to slur as he fought the effects of the medica-tion. "I have to leave you, Lydia. There are things I can't do...and be...with...you. But I will...always...love you." His eyes flut-tered shut.

"Jacob! Jacob, wake up!" She shook him, but he didn't move. "And I will always love you, too...Elisha."

# # #

She staggered into the flower garden between the hospi-tal lobby and the parking lot. Night inched across the sky toward the thinnest sliver of crescent moon in the pink shades of retreat-ing daylight. The new moon. Beginnings.

The grass felt cool and wet under her sore feet. She needed a jacket but the chill no longer bothered her. In her mind, she thanked the Goddess for a man who loved her and was noble enough to put the world's safety ahead of their togetherness. She thanked the Goddess, too, for his health because the car accident certainly could have gone much worse. Finally, she thanked the Goddess for allowing Jacob to understand Lydia's "differences" at last, even though his understanding hadn't brought them together, but had separated them forever.

"Whatever you send out," someone said from behind her, "comes back to you times three."

Lydia didn't turn to face the owner of the voice. She knew it was Maddie behind her. "You came to gloat? To say you told me so?"

"Never. I came to offer comfort."

"I don't think that's possible."

"Lydia." Maddie stood beside her then, no longer in a 1970's nurse's uniform but in a sheath of purple. Her blonde hair gleamed silvery-white at her shoulders. Crows' feet at the corners of her eyes belied an age difference of at least ten years from her last appearance. "My oldest friend. Don't despair."

Lydia sniffled. "How can you expect anything else? I did the same as my mother, maybe worse. I broke my own ethical standards for my own selfish reasons. I wanted Jacob to understand my visions so he could understand me. I'd thought it would bring us closer together. Instead…instead of being with me, he had to follow those visions to a life away from me."

"You can't tamper with someone else's destiny without permission and not pay the price."

Lydia turned to look Maddie full in the face. *The Lorelei.* "But you do it," Lydia realized. She thought back on what she'd seen, both in the physical realm and in her visions. "You do it all the time! When Jon was born, you helped Jacob get in to see me. When I was going nuts in that mental ward, you kept me company. When Mama was dying, you sent me to her. When I almost drowned in that stream, you sent Jacob to rescue me. When that idiot kid tried to blow up the school, you hauled him down to the police station. When I performed my ritual to give Jacob visions—" Lydia shook her head. She balled her fists and fought the urge to strangle the woman in front of her. "*You* tamper with people's lives *all the time!*"

"With permission."

"I never said you could tamper with my life."

"Yes, you did."

"Yeah? When? Who asked you to change the course of my life and Jacob's?"

"You did. Both of you." The Lorelei smiled. "In December of 1999."

Lydia blinked at her. Her future self had sent Lorelei back to change her course? "Then...then why aren't Jacob and I together?"

"Before you were born, you made some choices. Your mother was right. Your lifelines were meant to intersect only once—when Jon was born—but your mother interfered and set your life on a different course. You and Jacob were meant to lead separate lives, accomplish separate missions. You weren't meant to be together, but you will be. And he will understand your spirituality and love you as much as ever."

Lydia pulse raced. "When?" How long would she have to wait? A month? Six months? A year?

"Years, Lydia. *Years.* That's the price to be paid for tampering with someone else's fate. But it will come. When the time is right."

"And...Jon?" She was almost afraid to bring it up. She reeled to face the moon as it swung lower on the horizon. "My mother bound him from understanding my magick. The binding holds. I've lost both Jacob and Jonathon."

"No, Lydia," the Lorelei said from behind her. "Your mother's binding will last only until a stronger witch comes along to undo it. Make sure you teach me well, because I'm that witch."

Lydia whirled in surprise, but the Lorelei was gone. Sparks shimmered in the air in a perfect oval gate. A portal of time and space.

Sighing, Lydia turned back to the crescent moon. She'd watched it wane to darkness and be reborn this night. This moon too would wax to fullness and wane again only to be reborn. The cycle, over and over. And one day, just as her perfect witch moons had always waned and started anew, so would her life with Jacob...*Elisha.*

She nodded to herself. Things were not as she wanted,

but they were as they had to be. And until she and her love could be together again, watching the changing of the moon would be enough.

Her covenant with the Goddess.

A reminder of what was.

A promise of what would be again.

The truest of love.

###

Also available from Spilled Candy Books...

Access by Lorna Tedder
The Sequel to Witch Moon Waning,
featuring Lorelei Madison Steele and Jonathon Colter

Read an excerpt now--

"I've spent almost every waking hour by your side, hoping something would happen. And it did."

No, it didn't, she wanted to say. She'd made damned sure nothing had happened between them.

"I watched you take on the world, Madison. You throw this impenetrable wall up around you and don't let anything get through to you. But I saw the cracks. I didn't want to. I didn't mean to. But they were there. I'd been in lust with you, but then I started to fall in love with you. With the real Madison, not the L. Madison Steele in your signature block."

"You saw the real me, huh?" she joked. "If you know what's good for you, you'll keep your mouth shut."

"Forget the tough guy image. I know you. I know there's a vulnerable side."

She shifted on the bed. "I don't want to get into this."

"I'm already into it with you. They say that sometime during our sleep, we let the masks we put on for the rest of the world fade and we let our true faces show. Back when I was helping you with the Cashwell baby, that first night I heard you crying in your sleep, you pierced my heart."

Madison let out a shaky breath. He was so wonderfully candid--probably a side-effect of his youth. Most men she knew wouldn't be caught dead displaying their hearts. Jon had a way of opening his own and crow-barring his way into hers, too.

"Do you...do you still want me?" he whispered low enough that if she said no, he could lie and claim he'd asked something else.

The old yearning she'd banished long ago stirred low in her stomach. She'd wanted him the moment she had first laid eyes on him. Right now, she wanted him even more.

Tim had been the heat beneath her winter. Warmth and passion. Somehow she'd always thought of him as summer, even though they'd fallen in love in early autumn and he'd been banished before the last spring freeze. When he'd left, her life had turned to winter. A barren, cold place where she was bent on survival and no time for the frivolity of magic and sunshine.

Jon. He wasn't summer to her, but maybe a little bit of spring. The thaw had begun.

Madison twisted her ring and gave it a gentle tug. What was the point of wearing Tim's ring when he hadn't cared enough in seven years to come back and claim her? Jon was right about that, too. She wasn't the same woman she'd been back then. That woman didn't exist anymore. She was no more the woman Tim remembered than Tim was the same man she'd fallen in love with. That Tim was dead. He had to be. Because if that Tim were still alive, he would have come for her long before now.

She pulled harder at the ring. She'd worn it for so long, she wasn't sure it would come off at all. If she pried off the shackle Tim had left on her finger, Jon could overlook the hurt of playing second lieutenant to her first. She kissed the tips of two fingers and pressed them against his lips. "Don't go anywhere," she whispered.

He closed his eyes and smiled.

Madison scurried into the bathroom and turned on the faucet marked "C." It took a spurt of steam for her to remember that "C" stood for "chaud" instead of "cold." She reversed the motion and turned on the "F" faucet, which spewed out freezing cold water.

She soaped her knuckle and pulled harder. Outside, Jon waited for her with his chiseled cheekbones and thin lips, with his slim hips and broad shoulders, with his gray-blue eyes of curiosity and fire, with his slender hands. And she was keeping him waiting.

Madison yanked on the ring until her knuckle turned white. It was almost as if her bones had grown around the ring as a tree trunk grows over a wire meant to support its structure and makes the wire a permanent part of its whole. Tim was a part of her past and her past was a part of her. She could no more erase Tim from her life than she could cut out her heart. Wrenching the ring from her finger wouldn't change anything except to give her another scar, a physical one.

She rinsed the last of the soap from her finger and dried her hands. Outside, Jon waited. Anticipation fluttered in her stomach. Tonight might be her last chance with him. If things went badly with Owen Plummer, there would be no second chance.

Rubbing her fingertips over her cheeks, she wished the dark circles would disappear. Her jaw still bore a slight yellowish bruise, courtesy of Dr. Frick. Her long hair, her beautiful hair Tim had loved, needed brushing and re-braiding. Her face badly needed a wheelbarrow's worth of make-up to give back the youthful glow that waned after nearly twenty-four non-stop hours. During the sleepless nights with Bronwyn Cashwell, Jon had seen her at her worst. Maybe one day, he'd see her at her best. It wouldn't be tonight.

She turned out the light and tiptoed back into the bedroom. Amid the dimness of distant city lights, she could see that Jon hadn't moved. He lay quietly atop the brocade bedspread, eyes closed, breathing softly.

Fast asleep.

She'd waited too long.

Madison kissed his forehead and tasted salt. She stood by his bedside and watched for a long time, memorizing the tired peace in his face, the curve of his eyelids, the smell of his skin after a travel-weary day. She filled her brain with enough of him to last the rest of her life, even if Owen Plummer put a bullet through her skull in the morning and her brain ceased to function. Given that, maybe she should concentrate on filling Jon's head with memories since he might keep his head longer, keep her memory alive along with himself.

Who the hell did she think she was?

She could wake him up with kisses and intentions of seduction. In a few days, he'd return to Eglin with a headful of sweet memories and a pair of empty arms. He'd struggle through every day and wonder as he pulled the sheets over him at night, whatever happened to his lover and when would she return? If she slept with him now, he'd spend the rest of his life pining for her.

She'd do to him what Tim had done to her.

Madison crossed to the window, pulled back the curtain, and stared out at the distant lights. She laid her brow against the window pane and shut her eyes tightly. In a moment of weakness, in the stillness of what she'd refused to recognize as love, her eyes stung. Hot tears seeped from under her lashes.

Sniffling, she backhanded the tears and steeled her spine. L. Madison Steele cried for no one.

Especially not herself.

Copyright 1999 Lorna Tedder

Also available from Spilled Candy Books...

The Temple of the Twelve
by Esmerelda Little Flame

Read an excerpt now--

As night fell, Caroline gazed at the New Moon, a soft crescent in the sky, whispering the incantations she had learned at her grandmother's knee...words of praise and adoration and power in the Light...and the Dark. Long before the moon had fully risen she was sitting in her chair, clutching her sketchbook in tight fists. Wondering what the Lady would think of the picture...desperately wanting to please...wanting so badly to know what the Lady would ask of her...simply hungering to see the face of Black again.

And when the Black came again...she didn't knock this time. The little room was filled with her presence and a dark silver mist she emerged out of. "Blessings, Caroline," she said softly.

Trying with all her strength to stay controlled this time, Caroline knelt. "My Lady," she said. This was all, but it was everything. Mine, she thought fiercely. Mine to adore, to serve. To love. Mine.

The Lady looked out at the crescent moon shining down on her, then turned back to Caroline and said, "It is the New Moon. In the name of the Twelve I ask, are you willing to accept your first task, given to you from the depths of blackness, from the depths of infinity?"

Caroline swallowed hard, then said in a choked voice, "I am willing."

As she knelt there awaiting her first task as a novice to be told to her, the Lady suddenly said, "What is in your hands?" Caroline held forth the sketchbook, not able to meet the black eyes. When the slender white hands of the Lady clasped it, an electric current ran through Caroline and made her cry out. It wasn't pain...it was simply power.

The Lady smiled at her. "There is magic here," she said simply, "deep in these pages."

Caroline thought she would die or go mad from the sheer joy that consumed her at those words. "For you, Lady," she managed, out of lips gone suddenly dry.

The Lady gazed for a long while on the sketch. Her aristocratic face was expressionless and still. When Black desires to show nothing...she shows nothing. Wordlessly she laid the sketch pad on the little table, then said, "I am the color of selfhood. I am the deepest place within you. Enveloped in me, you become able to see more truly. I am often described as a place where you can hide the truth or hide from the truth. This is why people fear me...because they fear themselves.

"Caroline. In the darkness you see with all senses...you use touch and smell and taste to see. Your entire being sees, not just your eyes. Therefore, the first task for any novice who seeks to serve me is to be able to see in the dark. To be able to see with all of yourself, without lies.

"For you, Little Bird, that place of true seeing lies somewhere in the land between your heart and your hands, when you draw and paint. At those moments you are the most yourself. Therefore...Little Bird, I charge you in the name of the Artist of all life, whose servant I be, to draw with those hands and with that heart which is within you--your own image.

"But not just your body, Little Bird. You must draw your soul, as completely and fully as you are able. Put into each line and shading your essence and spirit. Draw the real you beneath all masks.

"And be aware, Caroline of the forest, that I can see in the dark. If you hide from yourself, if you hide from me, if in your work I see that you have not reached as far into yourself as you are able--then you shall try again in the next moon, and the next, and the next, and the next, until you either succeed or give up trying. For I tell you that no other of the Twelve shall appear to you unless I bid them entry.

"Be aware, you who seek to enter the Temple of the Twelve, that many do not pass out of the darkness of this first task. Child, there is a woman of seventy-one years who has been trying to do this since her girlhood. She does not give up. So I return to her. Again. She lives now among you, in the Temple grounds, though she has married, and so lives in a little cottage in the sacred woods with her husband, himself a priest of colors, although one who has not passed through the earliest levels after his novitiate years.

"Caroline of the forest, Little Bird, knowing that I shall see all lies, do you still desire to walk this path?"

"Yes, my Lady, I do."

"A third time I ask, for I always ask thrice, do you accept my challenge and my request of you?"

"With all my soul."

"So mote it be. I shall see you again, child, on the night before the next New Moon. Until then, I bless you in the name of the One." And the Lady raised up her hands, smoke and mist rose up all around her, and when it cleared, she was gone...leaving Caroline holding her sketchbook in her hands, not sure at all how it got there.

c2001 by Esmerelda Little Flame

Also available from Spilled Candy Books...

Once Upon a Beltane Eve
by Selene Silverwind

Read an excerpt now--

Julian scanned the grounds. "I've never done that before," he said, pointing toward a Maypole.

"Then we'll do that. There's one starting in a minute."

As they walked to the pole where several revelers were already gathered, he asked Fiona how long she had been Wiccan.

She glanced over at him. "Oh, I'm not."

"But you seem to know so much about this"

She laughed. "I guess I do have a lot of Wiccan tendencies. My parents had several Wiccan friends in Old San Francisco. That's where I'm from. We adopted a lot of their practices, but my family never formally studied the faith. I am Pagan, though."

"There's a difference?"

Fiona nodded and launched into the explanation she had heard some of her Wiccan friends give. "Paganism encompasses many earth-based faiths. Wicca is just one of them. Kind of like being Lutheran or Catholic. They're both Christian religions, but they're not the same."

They arrived at the pole and joined the circle that had already formed around it. Fiona walked to the middle and carried the ends of the two remaining ribbons back to the edge of the circle that had already. Fiona handed Julian a blue one, then he turned away from her to face the same direction she faced. She gently placed her hand on his shoulder, turning him toward her. "The men go widdershins, the women go deosil." Seeing the confusion in his eyes, she clarified. "Counterclockwise and clockwise. You go under the first woman's ribbon and then over the next, or at least you try. We keep dancing until the ribbons run out."

The High Priestess called the circle to order and they

turned to face the center of the circle. She explained that the pole was a symbol of fertility, then asked the participants to make a wish for something they wanted to manifest in the coming year, then send it into their ribbons. The revelers went around the circle stating their wishes aloud. Fiona wished for success in new friendships, blushing and casting a sidelong glance at Julian. He grinned and wished for the same thing. After the last man had stated his wish, the High Priestess wished that all the attendees would see their desires granted during the next year. The participants bowed their heads in silence, empowering the ribbons with their desires.

After a moment, the High Priestess began to sing the Maypole chant. The dance started slowly as the participants worked out a rhythm. The dancers' speed increased as the ribbons were woven into a multi-colored braid around the pole. The circle became tighter. When the ribbons reached their ends, the accompanying dancers tied them to the pole. They stepped outside the circle to watch those that remained, and aid them in the dance by clapping along to the beat of the chant. Those who knew the words sang along with the High Priestess. With the removal of some of the dancers, the over/under pattern lost its rhythm. Laughter erupted inside the circle and the dance became a chaotic jumble of confusion. Julian tried to maintain a steady pattern, while Fiona allowed her dance to disintegrate into a free-form frolic. Julian's ribbon reached its end before Fiona's. He stepped away to wait for her as she continued weaving her ribbon down to its last inch with a determination he admired. When her ribbon ran out, she left the circle, panting, and went to stand next to Julian to catch her breath. The dance was down to two last merrymakers. When they could wrap no more, they tied the ribbons together to lock in the desires of all the dancers.

Overwhelmed by the joy permeating the celebration, Julian grabbed Fiona, then swung her around in an impulsive hug. She looked into his laughing eyes and tilted her head down, her lips meeting his with the fleeting touch of a hummingbird, then again with more pressure. Their lips had never met before in this lifetime, but they knew the geography of each other in an instant, recognizing each other from the kisses of lifetimes past.

c2001 by Selene Silverwind

Want more?

Order Form

Check the appropriate block & circle format desired.

Witch Moon Rising, Witch Moon Waning
____Ebook Download (rtf, pdf, or html) $5.95
____Ebook Diskette (rtf, pdf, and html) $6.95
____Trade Paperback $13.95

Access
____Ebook Download (rtf, pdf, or html) $5.95
____Ebook Diskette (rtf, pdf, or html) $6.95
____Trade Paperback $14.95

Once Upon a Beltane Eve
____Ebook Download (rtf, pdf, or html) $5.95
____Ebook Diskette (rtf, pdf, and html) $6.95
____Trade Paperback $15.95

The Temple of the Twelve
____Ebook Download (rtf, pdf, or html) $5.95
____Ebook Diskette (rtf, pdf, or html) $6.95
____Trade Paperback $17.95

Shipping/Handling FREE using this form

Total: $

Name:

Address:

Email Address:

(More on back)

Mail to: Spilled Candy Books, P O Box 5202, Niceville FL 32578

___Check_____Money Order ____Credit Card (Visa/MC)

Card #

Expiration Date   Card Type

Name on Card:

Signature:

For More

Spilled Candy Books,

visit

www.spilledcandy.com

We offer free articles on spirituality, free excerpts of our books, a free ezine, a free ebook of magickal recipes, and books by some of the best spiritual authors on Earth.

We are truly blessed....find out why by visiting our web site or asking your local library or bookstore to order our books for you.

*ATTN religious organizations--if you plan to use our books in teaching circles, please write Spilled Candy for special discounts.

Brightest blessings!